Double Dog Dare

Argentina Ryder

Contessina Publishing

Contents

Chapter One

"Tell me, what else has been going on with you besides having a big deadline at work?" Aunt Linda's face, full of deep frown lines and bushy brows, filled Luke Granger's computer monitor screen and peered forward, as if she could look down at the keyboard on his messy desk. "You haven't stopped typing since we started video chatting with each other today. You know how I feel about that," she said, disappointment in her tone.

Luke's face froze, his hazel eyes darting from his keyboard to her face. *I probably should have canceled today's check-in,* he thought, and stopped typing. But Luke had postponed the last few times Aunt Linda wanted to chat, and she would have read more into that than the simple truth—business was booming, and Luke was busy. Nonetheless, their weekly check-ins were important; at least, that's what she often reminded him.

He minimized the window on his second monitor and focused his attention on his aunt. One hand reached up and pushed shaggy brown bangs out of his face. He needed a haircut. "I'm sorry, Aunt Linda. You have my full attention."

Linda leaned back in her own chair, her face now warm and compassionate, and her crooked smile reminded Luke of his mother. She adjusted her laptop and tucked a strand of graying brown hair behind her ear. "I understand that your work is important, and I don't want to take up too much of your time. Do you have a strict deadline coming up?" she asked and looked behind Luke, trying to scan his bedroom.

Luke shrugged, and with one finger carefully slid the webcam toward a cleaner part of the room, away from the pile of dirty clothes and stacks of books and graphic novels. "No more than normal. The hardest part about freelance work is the discipline it takes to get projects completed on time when there's no big boss around to check on your progress. If I cannot meet my deadlines, I receive no payment."

She sat in her kitchen just outside of Chicago, a thousand miles from him in Houston, Texas. "That makes sense. Can you tell me about what you're working on?" she asked.

Behind her, Luke spotted a rooster canister set on her countertop that once belonged to his mother. Luke pushed away a flitting memory of the two of them baking cookies when he was little, flour and sugar and those roosters. That was a long time ago. "It is a mobile fitness application for people training for marathons and other long-distance running. The app has been out for almost a year, but they have asked me to configure some needed updates to improve performance." It was one of Luke's favorite projects, and he was proud of how successful the application ended up. His fingers itched to open the screen back up and get back to work. "If you ever decide to take up jogging as a hobby, I highly recommend downloading it and giving it a try."

Linda laughed. "Maybe I'll look into it." Her dark eyes darted around again as she examined Luke's workspace. "So, I guess you're still working from home. Still in your bedroom."

This question, every time. "It works better for me, and I don't see what difference it makes where I work. I make my deadlines." Some people weren't made for a nine-to-five office schedule—Luke learned that long ago. "I see nothing wrong with this decision, as long as I can maintain my work responsibilities."

But Linda had her reservations and continued to voice them each time they talked. "How many people did you speak to in the last week? Real life people, not just someone in an internet chatroom, or across a screen like this," she said, and waved her finger back and forth at the two of them.

Hmm. "I went to the store on Tuesday, so there were people there. I didn't leave the house on Wednesday or Thursday, and I saw the dentist on Friday. Jessica had some work friends over here last weekend, and I hung out with them for a while."

Not that Luke didn't like people, not really.

He just preferred staying home, away from sizeable crowds. Away from strangers.

His mother had called him her little homebody. His pediatrician had another name for it.

A soft chime on his phone went off. *Reminder: Junebug's appointment at vet.* Oh no, there wasn't any chance that Luke would have forgotten that. Just the thought of spending time with the world's most handsome veterinarian had his pulse racing. "Also, I will take our latest foster dog out to the vet's office later this afternoon."

Aunt Linda smiled at that, satisfied that Luke wasn't hiding away from the world—at least not this week. "Luke, I know you think I'm a pain in the ass."

"Aunt Linda, I would never—" Luke said, and pushed back the guilt at making his mother's sister feel this way. Yet at the same time, he really wanted to get off this call.

But she knew what was up. "No, you'd never tell me to my face. And I know you only put up with these chats because of the trust."

She was wrong, but Luke didn't have the time nor the desire to argue. He had been nineteen and in college when his parents suddenly died, and while they hadn't been exceedingly wealthy, their house and some other property and annuities left for him and Jessica had been placed in a trust, currently managed by Aunt Linda. When Luke turned thirty, the property and the annuities fell into their hands to do with as they pleased.

Three years left. Three years of placating Aunt Linda, who insisted that Luke's introvert tendencies were just as dangerous as Jessica's daredevil attitude. "I enjoy talking to you," Luke murmured, and ran a hand through his wild brown curls. Even though it was June in Houston, he pulled his flannel shirt around him tighter. "You're the only family we have left."

That got her attention. "And I only want what's best for you two. I wish we lived closer, so I could check in with you in person, but this—" Linda pointed at the screen. "This is the next best thing. And I do appreciate you talking to me." Her face twisted in worry. "I don't suppose Jessica's around. I haven't talked to her in almost a month."

Oops. Luke's little sister wasn't as conscientious as he was about keeping up with these calls. "She's not home right now. I believe she's at work."

Linda didn't like that answer. "I follow her social media accounts. I see the danger that she gets herself into, sneaking onto other people's property and stealing their dogs."

Luke shook his head. "She's saving lives, Aunt Linda. Many of those animals are abandoned or abused, and people call her rescue organization because those animals need help." But even Luke hated the dangerous methods Jessica sometimes utilized, even worse when her sidekicks recorded and uploaded their escapades for everyone to see.

Aunt Linda snorted. "She's twenty-five years old. She should finish college and get a proper job, not spend her time stocking groceries."

Luke frowned. "She enjoys her job, and volunteering for the rescue organization makes her happy."

Aunt Linda was silent for a moment. Then– "I know losing your parents so young affected both of you. The same trauma that drives her to these risky behaviors causes you to self-isolate so that you don't have to experience those personal connections to people who you might lose."

Oof. Aunt Linda married a therapist five years ago and had picked up a lot of the lingo. "I haven't isolated myself," Luke mumbled.

"Haven't you?" Her face softened, and she reached out and touched the screen. "I worry about you two. I made a promise to my sister that I'd watch over her children."

Game, set, match to Aunt Linda. "I'll tell Jessica to call you later. I promise. And—" Luke scrubbed his face with his hand. "I'll speak with her about the dog stuff." He took a deep breath, and admitted, "It concerns me as well."

Aunt Linda smiled. "That sounds good. I'll talk to you next week, okay? And good luck today at the vet's office."

If Aunt Linda noticed Luke's face turning red at the mention of the vet, she said nothing.

Good. His idiotic crush wasn't a topic he wanted to bring up with anyone. *Ever*.

Chapter Two

The smell hit Chance Edwards as soon as he opened the door to exam room two. "Oh wow. That's—"

Sad bleating sounds, made by the sticky and stinking cat sitting on the exam table, broke his heart. "Nothing I tried at home worked. I Googled everything I could, and I think it's gotten worse." The tear-stained face of Mrs. Cavazos, the cat's owner, turned toward Chance, and her plump frame shook as she sniffled. "Rajah never gets out. She's always a good girl. But somehow, she escaped last night, and this morning, she was at the back door, with that nasty stuff all over her."

Rajah's usually sleek white fur was covered in a thick, dark goo that reeked. Chance reached for a pair of gloves and pulled them on, then glided one finger along her back. He took a sniff and wrinkled his nose. "I'm not sure what it is, but it feels oil-based." After a quick examination to make sure that there were no other injuries, he called Norma, the clinic's vet tech, to join them. "Let's get Rajah into the bathing station. Five milligrams of Acepromazine if she needs sedation." Turning back to Mrs. Cavazos, Chance pulled off his gloves and threw them in the trash. "We can get her soaking in something that will dissolve this goop, but it might take a while. Do you want to come back later today to pick her up?"

Mrs. Cavazos nodded, her shoulders slumping, and after Norma took the cat from the exam room, he spent another moment with Rajah's tearful owner. "Are you all right?"

She touched the corners of her eyes. "I'm sorry. I'm fine. It's just—I know it sounds stupid, but this was just the last thing I needed this week. First the car's battery died yesterday, and I had to get a new one. Then I got called by the school because my son was in a fight, and they sent him home. Now my car reeks of whatever Rajah rolled in." She scrubbed her face with her hand. "Do you ever have one of those days you wish you'd just stayed in bed?"

Oh yes. *If you only knew.* "The good news is that when you get back, we'll have gotten most of that off her. She isn't hurt or sick, like several of the other animals that come in here. She's just... stinky."

They both laughed, and Mrs. Cavazos nodded. "You're right. It could be much worse." She smiled and looked up at him. "Thanks for helping her."

After she left, Chance headed to the back of the Westgate Animal Hospital and entered the large room with the oversized sink where they bathed the animals. Leaning against the door, he examined a stain on his blue scrubs. He'd probably need to change before the next patient. "How's it looking?" he asked.

Norma's wrinkled nose spoke volumes, but it looked as if the sedative had taken effect. The cat lay quiet in the sink as the older woman scrubbed her efficiently, but with obvious care and affection. "This is the worst shit I've ever seen a cat get into, and I've been doing this for almost twenty years."

Gigi, the clinic's receptionist, poked her head in the room, her long red curls bouncing on her shoulders. "Dr. Edwards, our eleven o'clock appointment just canceled."

Chance nodded at Gigi in thanks. "Well, I guess I can help you out here with Miss Rajah for a few minutes. Have we figured this smell out yet?" he asked Norma and pulled on a fresh set of gloves.

Norma grunted. "I found a few fish bones and scales in her fur, so I'm guessing she ran across a carcass somewhere. Something that died and rotted in the summer sun."

Chance frowned. "While we've got her quiet, we might as well check for fish bones in her mouth."

Norma glanced down at her bright pink scrubs, damp and stained with whatever was on the cat. "I hope I can get the smell out; these were my favorites."

Before Chance could respond, his phone vibrated. But one glance at the name on the message was all he needed to see. The phone went back into his pocket.

Norma laughed and used her arm to wipe her face. "Are you avoiding someone, Doctor Chance? It must be bad if washing a stinking cat is preferable."

The cat shampoo was thick and smelled medicinal. "Sort of. It's my mother."

Norma's face fell. She'd worked with Chance long enough for her to know all about Chance's rocky relationship with his mother. "Still not any better?"

"No," Chance whispered. "Nothing's changed. I'm fine. She's fine. And yet—"

Nothing set Chance's teeth on edge quite like a family function. He avoided them like the plague.

But that was hard for some people to understand, people who grew up surrounded by love and acceptance. Norma always hoped things would work out for him one day. "She loves you."

Chance shrugged. "She loves Donovan Chance Edwards IV, Doctor of Veterinary Medicine." The successful son, tall and handsome, with movie star looks and a brilliant brain to match. That ideal man, that's who she loved.

But Chance never felt like that, her personification of his best qualities. Most of the time he was just Chance, a goofy dude who liked animals and dated men.

Hell, there wasn't even much of that anymore. Chance couldn't remember the last time he went out on an actual date.

"She'll come around one of these days." Norma held on to her hopes for a happy ending, and Chance loved her for that.

"I hope so," he murmured, turning off the tap as Norma bundled Rajah into a thick blue towel and carried her off to the cat crates to dry off.

Avoiding his mother's calls wasn't how Chance wanted to spend the rest of their lives.

A couple of hours later, the rush of morning patients died down. Time to find out what was going on with Mom. The lights were off in the office Chance shared with his clinic partner, Dr. Clara Berry, but that was okay.

The cool and quiet darkness suited his mood. Sitting at his desk, Chance looked up and saw his diplomas. He was a strong, educated man who shouldn't balk at the idea of standing up to his mother.

That was the plan.

The phone rang twice before his mother picked up. "Chance?" she said sweetly.

A good mood today, that was encouraging. "Hi Mom. Sorry I missed your call."

"Oh, I understand. I don't like calling you at work, but I wasn't sure if you had the morning shift or the evening shift."

Marcia Edwards sounded out of breath. Probably out shopping, he mused. "That's all right. Is everything okay?"

"Oh yes, I just wanted to check and see if you wanted to ride with your father and me to the wedding in Beaumont this weekend, or if you were going on your own." Despite her bright tones, there was steel in her words, an insistence that brooked no argument.

Wedding? Oh, yeah. Bridget and Mason. "I already talked to them—I can't make it." The silence on the other end lasted long enough that Chance asked, "Are you still there?"

That soft-as-butter tone turned icy cold. "Bridget is your cousin, Chance. Why aren't you going to her wedding?" Marcia demanded.

Chance leaned back in his office chair and rolled his eyes. "I went to her first wedding, isn't that enough?" he asked as he played with his computer mouse.

"Chance." His mother's tone was sharp.

His eyes closed. "Sorry, Mom. I've got something else happening this weekend, and I can't get out of it. I'm needed. Besides, when was the last time I even spoke to Bridget?" *Probably her last wedding*, Chance almost said, but his mother wouldn't think that was funny. "I sent them a nice present. An air fryer. A big one."

"What are you doing that's more important than your family?"

Here we go. "We're holding our annual fundraiser for the Pride Center. I told them I'd be there." Even over the phone, Chance heard the tsk sound she made whenever he mentioned the Pride Center and his volunteer work with the organization. But today, that sound emboldened him. "Can I put you down for a donation?"

"Don't be silly." His mother snapped at him, then her voice dropped. "You know it will disappoint your father that you're not coming this weekend."

And there it was, the pointed stab to make Chance feel guilty. "I know that. And I'll call him later and talk to him." Despite the rocky relationship he had with his mom, Chance had never had issues with his father–other than his father's unwillingness to stand up to his wife on his son's behalf.

But she wasn't done. "I'm disappointed that you're putting those people before your own flesh and blood."

Chance didn't argue; they'd had this discussion many times. His life was an endless roller coaster, always disappointing one person or another. Chance never felt like he did enough. His parents wanted more, the dog rescue organization he worked with needed him more than ever, and now these connections he made at the Pride Center were in danger because he couldn't follow through on his commitments to them.

And people wondered why he didn't have a boyfriend. He'd be just one more person for Chance to disappoint.

What a great online profile: Chance Edwards–six foot one, blond hair, blue eyes, a decent body and yet–never quite good enough.

Never quite good enough.

Time to end this conversation. This time, Chance chose the Pride Center fund raiser. "I'm sorry to disappoint you, Mom."

Marcia's voice dropped, almost a whisper. "I'm sorry too. I thought I had raised you better than that."

Before Chance could respond, the call ended. "Okay then."

That went well.

Chapter Three

The Westgate Animal Hospital sat in a small two-story shopping center close to midtown, nestled between a dog groomer and a coffee shop. It was a lively pedestrian area, with a popular Greek restaurant across the street and some trendy clothing shops next door.

The parking lot was half-full when Luke pulled up in his Subaru Forester with Junebug harnessed in the back. He parked and sat in his car for a minute and took a few deep breaths. A quick glance in the small mirror on the sun visor assured him he looked presentable; hair combed and face washed.

Not that it mattered, but there was no sense in showing up looking like some slob.

A whimper from the backseat pulled him from those dark thoughts. "Almost ready. I'm just—"

I'm just what? Primping? Talking myself up before I head inside? Voices in his head told him this was stupid, and yet, it happened each time Luke brought a foster in for some medical attention.

Because he had a crush on the vet.

Even worse, Luke was almost certain that his sister arranged all their dog appointments on days when Doctor Chance was on duty, but he hadn't been able to verify that.

Today's special dog was Junebug, a playful beagle rescued from a local kill shelter, who Luke and Jessica were fostering for a few weeks. Luke untethered her from the backseat, secured her harness and set her on the ground, then walked her inside the clinic. Her leash skills had improved, he noted.

A quick glance and Luke saw that the vet clinic was almost empty as he approached the front desk. "Good morning."

"Good morning, Mr. Granger." Gigi's bright smile always put him at ease. She peered over the counter. "I see we've got Miss Junebug with us today?"

Luke cleared his throat. "Yes, she's staying with me for another two weeks. She requires a certificate of health before she heads off to her new rescue."

"Good for her." Gigi typed on her keyboard and then nodded. "Have a seat and I'll let them know you're ready."

Luke found some chairs on the far side of the waiting room, away from a yapping Chihuahua and a timid Dalmatian hiding under a chair. He and Junebug practiced sit and stay. "You're doing very well," he told Junebug and offered her a treat just as Norma, the vet tech, stepped out of the back area.

She smiled when her searching eyes spotted them. "Good afternoon. Are you ready?"

"Yes." Luke had been here many times with their various foster dogs and had the vet tech's routine memorized. First a stop at the large scale to get an accurate weight of the dog, then a vigorous scritch on the back of their heads and behind their ears, and finally taking them into an empty examination room where she'd document the animal's pertinent information for the visit. Luke had his foster dog binder with him as well, to assist him with keeping track of whatever information they gave him during that visit, along with a small bag containing a fresh stool sample.

Exam room three had posters of dogs at all stages of life, and an advertisement for heartworm medication. Luke closed the door behind him and unleashed Junebug. The beagle was small enough that they could easily lift her onto the exam table, where Norma's gentle, yet firm hands gave the dog a quick physical exam. "No lingering effects from her spay?"

"Nothing. Her incisions healed well, and the dissolvable stitches have—" Luke searched for the right word, but only came up with—"dissolved."

Norma grinned. "That's great news. And today we're here for the last round of shots before her transport?"

Luke's hand stroked her back and he rubbed the silky fur on her ears. "Yes. She's leaving in two weeks."

"Okay, I'll let Dr. Edwards know that you're in here."

Luke set Junebug back on the ground with obvious gentleness and let her sniff the room. "This will be much less stressful than last time we were here," he said in an assuring voice, and bent over to soothe the scared animal.

But the door opened, and Dr. Edwards stepped into the room. His familiar and gentle laugh told Luke that he'd heard Luke's comforting words to the dog. "I'm guessing Miss Junebug didn't like her last visit here?"

Luke's skin went prickly hot as he turned to face the veterinarian. Even in those plain blue surgical scrubs, Chance Edwards could have been a model or a movie star—he was *that* good looking. His perfectly combed golden hair and tanned skin would not have been out of place on a beach in California, holding a surfboard and drinking up the sunshine. "There was the small matter of her surgery. Or rather—" Luke's lips quivered with amusement. "—the surgical cone afterwards."

Dr. Edwards nodded in agreement. "Ah, she didn't like the cone."

Luke's eyebrow arched. "No one likes the cone, Dr. Edwards."

The vet's face broke out into a wide smile, his laugh like music. "You got me there, Mr. Granger." Dr. Edwards bent down on the floor and gave Junebug a quick pet, then lifted her back onto the table. "Norma tells me she's getting ready to head to a new rescue?"

Luke nodded. "Bradley's Beagle Rescue of Oregon. They're taking her in, and she'll be leaving at the end of the month, if her transport run gets filled."

"Oregon? That'll be fun, Junebug. Lots of gigantic trees and forests to explore. You'll like it there." As Dr. Edwards spoke, his hands skimmed her body, checking her legs, her teeth, and under her tail. "Have you ever been to Oregon, Mr. Granger?"

Luke shook his head and swallowed as he tried not to imagine those strong hands examining him—and utterly failed. "Alas, no," he said, and ran a hand through his hair.

"You should see it someday, especially in the summer. Trees everywhere, and not like the little ones we got around here. Real trees growing on the sides of mountains, taller than anything in Texas." Dr. Edwards flipped Junebug on her side and examined her spay incision spot. "This looks nice and clean. Great job taking care of her, as usual."

If they talked about the dogs, Luke's thoughts stayed focused. But as soon as Dr. Edwards turned his attention to Luke, the blithering idiot emerged. "We followed the instructions you gave us."

He nodded and caught Luke's eye. "To a tee."

Norma walked in, her curious eyes darting between the two of them. "Mr. Granger, did you bring the stool sample?"

Luke held up the bag of poop. She took it from him with a smirk and stepped back outside.

"As soon as we get the results from that test, I can complete her health certificate, and Miss Junebug here will be ready to hit the road." Dr. Edwards scratched behind her ear again. "Oregon. Lucky dog. Sometimes I wish—" But he stopped speaking and sighed instead. "How's your sister doing?"

Luke barely contained a snort. "Looking for trouble." Dr. Edwards worked with several rescue organizations and knew all about Jessica's activities.

"I saw a video she posted a few days ago. She and another man had pulled onto the side of Interstate 10 and were rounding up some strays that had gotten into traffic." He whistled low. "It takes guts to do what she does, go out there and find those lost animals. She has more patience than I have."

Luke shook his head. "Yes, but you heal them once she finds them. Without that medical attention, they wouldn't have any sort of quality of life." Dr. Edwards smiled at Luke's words, a thoughtful look on his face, as if he hadn't realized what seemed like a glaring truth to everyone else. "You're a hero, too." Their eyes met and locked until Luke turned away, suddenly uncomfortable. "Um, when will the health certificate be ready?"

Dr. Edwards pulled his phone out of his pocket. "If we get the sample to the lab today, it might be as early as tomorrow. I'll ask Gigi to let you or your sister know as soon as we get it."

"Thank you. Someone from the organization will be by." Luke reached down to clip Junebug's leash back onto her collar.

"I'll have it ready at the front desk." Dr. Edwards reached into a large plastic jar and pulled out a small dog bone. "A treat for an excellent patient." Junebug's large brown eyes widened as she accepted the treat from Dr. Edwards's hand, and she chewed it enthusiastically. "I guess this is our last visit with you, Miss Junebug. Your forever family is going to be lucky when they find you." Then he looked up at Luke again, that soft smile making his insides ache. "I hope to see you soon."

Luke's insides twisted; a queer feeling, simultaneously wanting to bolt as fast as he could, and yet—he never wanted to leave. Luke swallowed hard and composed himself. "Knowing my sister and her proclivities, I'm sure it won't be too long."

• • • • • • • • •

Jessica's ancient Ford Explorer was parked in the driveway when he and the dog pulled up to their house. Luke peered at the left back panel—was that a new dent? Jess's car carried the scars of the more adventurous side to her dog rescue activities. He walked Junebug into the house and took off the harness, setting her leash next to the front door.

A woman's voice called out from upstairs. "Is that you?"

A preposterous question, now an inside joke that Luke grudgingly played along with. "No, it's not me." Thunderous footsteps pounded down the stairs as Luke passed through the living room toward the kitchen. "The health certificate might be ready tomorrow."

Jessica caught up with Luke and fell into a chair next to the kitchen table, a golden retriever and a smaller black dog of mixed breed settling at her feet. In her trademark tank top and denim cut-offs, Jessica was always surrounded by dogs. She shared Luke's slender frame and curly brown hair with hazel eyes, but her small, turned-up nose gave her a roguish quality that matched her personality. "Toss me the dog bone box, will you?"

Luke picked up the box and handed it to her, then pulled a box of frozen French bread pizza out of the freezer. "Has Junebug's transfer run filled?" In addition to her forays in Houston's lower socioeconomic neighborhoods in search of dogs being mistreated, chained up, or used as backyard breeders, Jessica volunteered as a transport coordinator for Four Paws Caravan, a group that helped moved rescue animals across the country.

She shook her head at Luke before turning her attention back to the dogs. "Sit." Now all three dogs surrounded Jessica's feet, each sitting up excitedly at the prospect of a treat. After receiving their bones, they tore off toward the living area, each dog heading to their favorite spot. Turning back to Luke, she continued. "There's a couple spots in Utah, and one in Idaho that still needs to be filled, but we've got plenty of time."

Luke marveled at the organization behind these transport runs. Junebug would travel over two thousand miles in hour-long relays, completely run and operated by volunteers, and Jessica would oversee much of that trip from her computer in Houston.

An image popped into his head. Real trees growing on the sides of mountains, taller than anything in Texas. Suddenly, Luke was filled with a powerful urge to see them. "Have you ever thought about moving away from here?" he asked as he prepared his lunch.

Jessica's face wrinkled in dismay. "Why? We don't have any rent or bills—it's all taken out of the estate. What reason would I have to leave?"

Luke shrugged. "We've been here our whole lives." Their eyes met, and Luke recognized the anxiety they shared over leaving their childhood home. Despite being the older sibling, Luke remained in the bedroom he'd grown up in, and offered the master bedroom to Jessica, who now shared it with whichever of her foster animals were staying with them.

She shook her head. "I have no plans to leave. But you're the one with the great job. You could get an apartment somewhere." She quirked a brow. "Why haven't you left?"

Why hadn't he left? He ignored that thought because they both knew the reason. "You could get a good job too, if you focused on a career as much as you do on the volunteering." Luke heard Aunt Linda's words spouting out of his mouth—but she wasn't wrong. "Have you thought more about it?"

Her arms crossed in front of her chest. "I like working at the grocery store."

"No, you don't. But the hours are flexible, and no one asks about your other activities."

She turned to him with narrowed eyes. "What's this really about?"

"I have… concerns. About you." Betsy, the golden retriever, trotted back to the kitchen and settled at Jessica's feet. "About the dangers you and Maggie put yourself in. I'm afraid for you."

Jessica's eyes went dark but softened as Luke sat down next to her. "You don't have to be scared. I can take care of myself. And I always have back-up."

"One of these days, you might run into the wrong back-yard, Jess, and someone will be there to stop you from taking their dog."

She scoffed and rested her head on her chin. "Ninety percent of the time, there's no one living there anymore. These—I can't think of a word horrible enough to describe them—these wicked people move and leave their animals behind. They chained these dogs to trees, to fences, and there's no one taking care of them." Tears formed in the corners of her eyes. "How do I leave them there?"

Luke leaned back in his chair. "I understand. But I still worry."

"Well, don't. I'm careful." Jessica took a deep breath and stood up. Leaning down, she kissed the top of Luke's head. "I've managed to take care of both of us this far, haven't I?" Before leaving the room, Jessica turned around and smirked. "How was Doctor Chance today? He look tasty?" Luke ignored her and pulled out his phone. "I'll take that as a hell yes," she added with a slow smile, and headed up the stairs with all three dogs behind her.

Chapter Four

"Mr. Granger's been spending a lot of time here recently." Gigi pushed a mop through exam room three, sanitizing the floor for the following day and a new round of patients.

Norma snorted at the younger woman as she refilled the supply cabinets in each room. "He doesn't have control of when he comes. The animals and their needs drive his schedule."

But it was impossible for Chance to miss the knowing look that passed between the two women. "He and his sister are doing amazing work, volunteering their time and money to help those animals."

"I know." Gigi wrung out her mop, then pushed the bucket with her feet to the next room and begun the process again. "But you can't deny, Doctor Chance, that he has a little crush on you."

Chance scoffed as his mouth went dry. "I know nothing of the sort." But he shifted his body away from their faces, back to the computer screen in the back exam room where he continued to inventory the surgical supplies. "He's a nice guy."

"A *real* nice guy," Norma added. Great, she was jumping in on the conversation too. "I never hear him talk about if he's seeing anyone."

They weren't even being low key about this. Chance finished entering one last column of numbers into his spreadsheet and then turned in his rolling chair to face them. "What is happening here? Why are we talking about this?"

Gigi poked her head out of the room she was cleaning, her warm brown eyes twinkling. "He's so cute, with all that curly hair on his head. And the way he talks—he sounds so intense all the time, but then he smiles. And—I mean, it's obvious that he likes you, Doctor Chance. It's written all over the man's face. And—" Her face lit up as she grinned. "You seem a little smitten with him as well, if you don't mind me saying so."

Chance went still. "I don't know what you're talking about," he said, and closed the laptop. "Mr. Granger is a client, and our relationship has always been professional."

"But have you ever thought about making it more than professional?" Norma leaned against the door frame. "It's been a while since you've gone out with anyone. You should ask him out."

Unbelievable. "Do either of you even know if he's gay?" When they shook their heads, Chance snorted. "And what would that be like, if suddenly, if your veterinarian started coming on to you romantically, making you uncomfortable? What would happen then? We'd lose an important client, that's what would happen. Someone who, just like you said, brings patients in several times a month for their rescue organization." This entire conversation was ludicrous. "It's not worth the risk."

Neither woman spoke again, but Norma smiled knowingly at Chance. After Gigi headed back to the front of the clinic, she rested one hand on his shoulder as she walked by his computer station. "It seems pretty clear he does like you. And yes, Doctor Chance, sometimes it is worth the risk." Norma had been at this clinic even longer than Chance had, and he appreciated her thoughtful words—even if they were hard to hear. But she also recognized that this was a touchy subject for Chance and changed the conversation. "Are you staying long? You've had a long day, with Dr. Berry still on vacation."

Chance shook his head. "I've got a couple emails to write. Go ahead and lock everything up, and I'll go out the back door." They waved at him as they headed toward the front of the clinic, and soon the soft chime of the front door, opening and closing, told Chance they'd left the building.

His fingers tapped against the top of his laptop, and he took a few deep breaths. Had he been that transparent? Was it written all over his face, the way Luke made him feel? What was the word Gigi had used? *Smitten*. For fuck's sake, was there anything more unprofessional than for someone's medical practitioner to look smitten when the patient (or their caretaker) was around?

If only it wasn't true.

From the first time that Luke brought one of their rescue animals into the clinic, there had been an instant spark between them, with definite feelings on Chance's end. Lithe and angular, with soft brown curls and velvety hazel eyes, Luke Granger was a perfect contrast to Chance's blond hair, blue eyes, and muscular build. Luke's droll sense of humor and occasional off-beat comments made Chance laugh, and even if he weren't physically attracted to Luke, Chance enjoyed seeing him as a patient, maybe even as a friend.

Unfortunately, that attraction was real. It had been a long time since Chance wanted to spend time with someone, and not just for a quick hook-up. There was something different about Luke that appealed to Chance. But just as he told the ladies, it couldn't happen between them, not right now, and if he was as transparent as he feared, nothing was more important than keeping his guard up.

As fun and romantic as the ladies made it sound, the last thing that Chance needed was to fall in love with his client.

Chapter Five

Luke's favorite ice cream in the world was Blue Bell's Peach Cobbler. But it was a seasonal flavor and only in stock during the summer months, so whenever the grocery store close to their house had it for sale, he purchased as much as he could fit into their freezer.

The checkout girl seemed amused. "Are you having a party?" she asked, as she scanned the eight pints and three half gallon containers and handed them to the bagger to pack into Luke's reusable insulated grocery store bags.

He frowned. "No, this is for me. But mark my words, this particular flavor is exceedingly popular, and never lasts long in stock."

The girl—Gina, according to her name tag—considered Luke's words. "Maybe there's someone else doing the same as you, hoarding them away."

"Then I would applaud their intelligence and tenacity." The rest of Luke's groceries passed through the scanner, and he finished paying for them.

Gina handed him the receipt with a smile, holding it a fraction of a second too long before he tugged it away from her. "I'll have to try that flavor some time, if you ever leave some for us."

"You'd like it." Luke gathered his grocery bags and headed out toward his Subaru. Just as he got the last bag into the back seat, it hit him. *That was flirting.* She'd flirted with him, and like an idiot, he'd missed it. A quick analysis of the situation reassured Luke that he'd done nothing to instigate it, other than amuse her with his ice cream information. Still, it left Luke a little unsettled, how easily he'd missed that.

Just as soon as Luke turned the key, his phone went off. It paired with his vehicle's Bluetooth system and soon the sound of a phone ringing was everywhere. Luke lowered the volume and hit the green telephone icon next to the word 'Jessica—sister.' "Hello."

"I got a 911 situation. We're over on South Dorado near Westheimer. How soon can you be here?" She breathed loud into the phone, as if she were running.

Luke looked down at his groceries and frowned. "How 911 are we talking?"

"Might be life and death for this girl. I haven't seen a leg this bad in a long time. There's a bunch of them and we're getting them out, but this old girl needs to see a vet right now." There was a pause as she spoke to someone else at the scene. "Chance knows she's coming as soon as you can get her there."

The urgency in her voice startled Luke. Jessica over-dramatized a lot of situations, but at this moment, she sounded frantic. "Send me the address. I'm on my way."

Once Jessica texted the address to him, Luke pulled it up on his phone's map application and headed in that direction. Fifteen minutes later, he turned the corner of South Dorado Street. He drove slowly until he spotted the beat-up Honda minivan that belonged to Maggie, Jessica's partner in crime for these rescues. Luke parked behind it on the residential street and looked around. It was an older neighborhood with rundown houses and large, unfenced yards—just the sort that often had a dog or two chained to a fence for protection.

Cautiously, he stepped out of his vehicle. It wasn't the dogs that frightened Luke, but an angry individual with a weapon who might mistake him for a thief—and right now, they would not be incorrect.

But it sounded as if Jessica and Maggie had already talked to some neighbors. Jess waved Luke over towards her. "Hey. The neighbors said that the people who lived here moved a week ago and left dogs behind." Maggie stood next to Jess, her stocky frame providing some protection, but at the moment her phone was out, recording everything.

A sick sense of dread filled Luke. "How many?"

"Three females, and one of them just had a litter." They walked back into an overgrown and unkept backyard, filled with bushes and trash bags. He saw where the dogs had torn the bags open, most likely in search of something to eat. It disgusted him. "Where's the injured one?"

"Over there." Jessica pointed at a young Hispanic man sitting on the ground with a dog in his lap. "This is Carlos. They live across the street and sent a text to the rescue when they realized that the dogs were still back here."

"Hi." Up close, Luke realized this wasn't a man, but a teenager. Dark wary eyes stared back at him, but Luke understood. All he knew was this strange man was here to whisk these animals away. But once Luke saw the dog, he understood. A black lab, but very thin and small for her breed, with a gaping, open wound on her leg. Fur and skin had been torn or eaten away, exposing the infected muscle and bone underneath. "Oh, you poor thing." Luke looked back up at Jess. "I'll get her to the vet. Where are the others?"

"Maggie got them into the van. I didn't want to move this little lady any more than we had to, so I waited for you." She knelt and carefully wrapped the dog's leg in gauze.

Luke lifted her carefully into his arms. "Hello." The dog trembled, a brief flash of terror in her eyes. What must be going through her head, he wondered, and why was she not crying out in pain? "You're safe now." Luke knew she didn't understand him, but when the dog looked up at him and their eyes met, he swore he felt her tense body curl into him, an act of trust that humbled him.

Jessica walked behind them. "Carlos, you tell your mom that we're leaving now and they're going to be taken care of. Thank you so much for letting us know and helping us."

Carlos smiled back as they arrived at Luke's Subaru. "I'll tell her. I like dogs. My uncle's dog is having babies soon, and my mom said I could get one of my own."

Jessica froze, her eyes blinking closed at the boy's comment. Luke understood. The cycle never ended here in Houston. But now was not the time to preach for spaying and neutering pets. "I'm sure you'll take great care of your dog. Thank your mom again for letting us know about these girls."

Luke opened the back of the Subaru and quickly set up a wide cage he kept for these situations. Soon the injured dog was secured but panting faster now—she was in distress. "I'll call you when I get there."

Jessica hugged him. "Thanks for coming so fast." Maggie waved, and Luke set out for the vet's office.

· · · · • · • · · ·

"Twice in one week. Aren't we lucky?" Gigi held the door open as Luke carried the dog inside. But her smile dropped as she glimpsed the patient. "Oh sweetheart, what happened to you?"

Norma waved Luke straight to the back, past the regular exam rooms, and into the large examination area. "Doctor Chance is finishing with another patient. Here, let's clean this up." Though she was still scared, the trembling dog allowed herself to be tended to, big brown eyes that sensed that she was in a safe place. "Oh, this leg looks bad. I hope we can save it."

Dr. Edwards walked in and beelined for the dog. "What have we got here?" He glanced up quickly in Luke's direction, throwing him a quick "Hi," and then together with Norma, examined the wounds.

The dog whimpered and wriggled around. "Let's get her sedated so we can get a good look at that gash. Luke, can you come help me?"

Luke froze. *Was this the first time he called me by my first name,* he asked himself. But Luke didn't have long to ponder that, as the medical team immediately began working on the dog's leg. Luke stood next to Dr. Edwards and followed his lead, holding the Labrador steady as Norma injected her with medication.

It hurt Luke to watch them, removing necrotic muscle tissue and flushing the wound with sterile saline, but soon the leg was wrapped in a loose bandage. "Are you going to—" Luke began, but then stopped. What did you do for a gaping wound like that?

"It's better to leave it like this. The muscle will re-knit on its own, given time and rest." Dr. Edwards wiped his brow, then touched Norma's arm. "I think we can give her a day or two with antibiotics to see if she might heal on her own." He looked over at Luke. "Can you roll that IV stand toward me? The short pole next to the wall."

Luke turned and spotted it, then pushed it toward the exam table. "Doctor—"

"Call me Chance, please," he said as he hurried into a storage closet and returned a moment later with an IV bag.

Luke bit his lip and nodded. "Chance." The name sounded good rolling off his tongue. But that worry lingered. "Is she going to lose the leg?"

"I hope not. Now that it's clean, we can give her some nutrients and medication." He and Norma lifted the dog and settled her into a recovery cage. "She's the only one back here, so she'll get the best of care."

Luke let out that breath he'd been holding. "She'll be okay?"

Chance rolled his head around his neck and stretched his arms. "I hope so, but it's going to be a long night. She's extremely malnourished and we'll have to wait and see if the infection has spread anywhere else. We'll know more tomorrow once we see how she reacts to the medication." He looked over at a large round clock hanging on the wall before turning back to Luke. "Do you want us to call you when we know something?"

What?" I'm not leaving. Not yet anyway." Luke looked back at the dog. She looked so small now that she settled down in the cage, nestled in blankets except for her leg where the IV stuck out of her. "Can I—" Luke pointed at a chair near the cages. "Can I stay? Please? I won't be in the way; you have my word."

Chance just stared at him, and their eyes locked for a long moment. Eventually he nodded. "I'm going to see the other patients. Let Norma know if you need anything." The veterinarian washed his hands and headed into one of the exam rooms. Luke heard him apologize for the delay in their service and then pulled out his phone to let Jessica know what was going on.

That task completed, Luke reached his hand into the cage and ran his fingers over a patch of fur. "You've got the best doctor in the world," he whispered to the sleeping dog. "Doctor Chance can do anything."

Chapter Six

The office computer had an old keyboard, and the sound of the clicks pleased Chance as he typed up reports from the day's patients and the services provided. A soft rap at his office door caught his attention. He glanced up. "Yes?"

"The rooms are cleaned and prepped for tomorrow." Norma leaned against the door frame, with her arms folded in front of her. "He's still here, you know."

Of course. Luke would need more assurances before leaving the dog for the night. "How's she doing?" Norma's face told Chance all he needed to know—the black lab was still not out of the woods. "Okay, it's going to be one of those nights." Chance turned off the computer and glanced down at his watch. Half-past six in the evening. It wasn't often that they had unscheduled overnight guests in the clinic, but this wasn't the first time an animal would require that level of constant care, where someone was required to stay at the clinic most of the night.

Norma read his thoughts. "Do you want some company? I can let my daughter know I'll be late."

Chance shook his head. "No, I've got it. And I'll run upstairs for anything I need." But it had been a long couple of days. "How does tomorrow's schedule look?"

Her brow furrowed. "Busy, but Dr. Berry will be back tomorrow. I called her and switched your schedules, so she'll be here from seven-to-three in case you need to sleep in. Now you've got the noon-to-seven shift. She also offered to stay as long as we need her."

Perfect. "Norma, you're an angel. How do you always know how to take care of me?" Chance stood, stretched, and rolled his head around his shoulders, frowning when his bones cracked loudly. "I'll go talk to Mr. Granger. You and Gigi head home." Her quizzical glance told him she wasn't sure how that conversation would go. "We'll be okay, I promise. Enjoy your night and I'll see you both tomorrow afternoon."

Once they left, Chance locked the front door behind them, and headed back toward the back exam room where Luke's dog slept. He hadn't moved from the chair where he sat, settled next to the cage, and stared at something on his phone. "Mr. Granger—Luke, are you sure you want to remain? Not much is going to happen tonight, and I can call you if something changes. I'll be here with her."

Luke looked at the dog, his dark brows pinched together on his thin, pained face. "If it's okay, I'd like to stay a little longer." He set the phone down in his lap. "It's not about trust. I know you're the best. I just—" His eyes locked on the dog; a silent communication between them. "I don't want to leave her until I am certain she's going to pull through."

"I understand." And Chance did. Bonds like that sometimes happened in the blink of an eye between an animal and a person. It was beautiful and heartbreaking. "You can stay as long as you want."

Relief spread across Luke's face. "Thank you."

Chance pulled another chair from the break room and sat down next to him. "How's your sister? You mentioned that there were others at the scene."

"Just got finished talking to her," Luke said, and tapped his phone. "They found two others who were hungry, but in better condition, as well as eight puppies. They'll bring them in tomorrow or the next day after they get them bathed and fed and pull all of the fleas off them." Luke nodded at the snoozing black lab. "What happened to her leg, can you tell?"

It disgusted Chance that she'd lived even one day in that agonizing pain and hunger. She'd suffered for days, maybe a week with that injury. "I think something took a bite out of her, and the wound got infected." Chance wanted to say that she'd be fine, that they'd take care of her, but he couldn't make that promise. "If she makes it through the night, she's got a good chance of survival." Luke's eyes were dark and sad, but it was the best Chance could do.

Luke leaned his head against the cage and watched her sleep. "I will never understand how a person can be so cruel. If you don't want your dog, then just give them up. Even roaming the streets is better than being tied up with an injury that," he said, and pointed at the leg.

Chance couldn't stop staring at Luke as he spoke, his features alive and expressive. He wanted to reach out and push a wayward strand of hair out of Luke's flushed face. But Chance kept his hands in his lap. "If you're going to be here, you might as well get comfortable." Chance walked into his office, then rolled his high-backed upholstered office chair, along with Dr. Berry's chair, into the exam room near the dog. "Take this one." A thought struck Chance. "You've been here since noon. Are you hungry?"

Luke laughed. It was the first smile Chance had seen on his face all day. "A little, but I have some food in your fridge. I'd been at the grocery store when my sister called, and never made it home. Norma was kind enough to let me use your refrigerator so the dairy and frozen items wouldn't spoil. I can just heat up one of my microwave meals."

Chance made a face. "Don't do that. I've got some tortilla soup upstairs. There's plenty—I made enough for the whole week. Do you want some?"

Luke brightened and grinned. "I admit, that sounds better than a frozen pot pie. But what do you mean, upstairs?" Then a light went off, his eyes flashing. "You live here?"

Chance nodded. "Yes. I don't advertise it, but the space above the office is my home." He checked the time. "I need to run up there, anyway. Would you like to come with me or do you want to stay with her? I won't be long, maybe fifteen or twenty minutes."

"She'll be okay alone?"

Again, it was hard but Chance couldn't lie to him. "There's not much we can do for her, other than just be here. If something happened and she crashed—"

Luke understood. "I'm torn. I don't want to leave her alone, but I'm also curious where you live. Not in a creepy way," he added quickly. "I've just never seen that sort of arrangement. I assume it's like a big studio."

"It's pretty cool, yeah. I tell you what—stay here with her, and I'll give you a tour another time, I promise." Thank God Norma and Gigi were gone; Chance could just see their faces reacting to his offer.

Luke seemed pleased as well, and something inside Chance warmed at the interested expression on Luke's face. "Then I'll remain. And—and yes, I'd love some of that soup. But dessert is on me. Best ice cream you've ever had, I guarantee."

"The best? That's a bold statement," Chance said with a grin, and jotted down his personal cell number on the back of a scrap of paper fished from his pocket. "Just in case something happens while I'm upstairs."

Luke plugged it into his phone and Chance felt his own phone vibrate. "That's me. Just in case."

With one more glance at the sleeping dog, Chance headed toward the back exit of the office and back into the stairwell leading to his apartment.

It had been quite a while since Chance had stayed at the office this late without making a visit up to check on Sheba, as he reminded him loudly when he opened the front door to his large studio loft, his pride and joy.

One of them, at least. "Look, I didn't know I was gonna be gone this late. I'm sorry." Turning on the kitchen light, he opened the fridge and pulled out the last two containers of soup he'd made for dinner this week. A soft thump behind him caught his attention. "You're not supposed to be on the counter."

Solid black fur with large green eyes, Sheba stood as still as an ancient statue. "Meow."

Chance sighed. Another battle he lost. "I don't remember the part where I needed to check with you when I was out late." The cat's face remained impassive, but his head butted against Chance's hand when he offered it to the cat. He was forgiven. "How about I make it up to you with dinner?" His expression didn't change as Chance scratched behind his ears, but he gobbled up two fresh anchovies and followed Chance into the bathroom where he freshened up.

Once he was back in the kitchen, Chance packed up some spoons, napkins, and a couple soft drinks into a bag along with the soup. "Alexa, play Sheba's playlist." The loft filled with the soft sounds of Tchaikovsky's Swan Lake. "Volume level three."

One more head scratch as the cat jumped onto the sofa. "I'll be downstairs. Hopefully I won't be there all night."

A lie, but he was a cat—and probably didn't understand his words.

Chapter Seven

The clinic's break room had a table and small sofa, but by an unsaid mutual agreement, neither man wanted to leave the dog alone in her cage. Chance warmed up the soup and brought it to where Luke sat, close to the dog. He pulled a small stainless steel tray table next to them, and set utensils, soft drinks, and some garnishes for the soup. "I wasn't sure what your feelings were on cilantro."

"It's a controversial herb." But one that Luke enjoyed, so he took a handful and sprinkled it liberally on top of his soup, along with some tortilla strips and a squeeze of lime juice. "You prepared this?"

Chance nodded with a slow smile. "I did. It turned out pretty good, too, and I hope you like it."

"I'm sure I will. My typical diet contains far too much processed food and take-out. Neither Jessica nor I ever learned to properly cook." Luke groaned as he tasted the soup. "This is incredible."

Chance blushed. "I'll have to show you how to make it. Man cannot live on frozen pot pies alone." He took another spoonful. "So, it's just you and Jessica? No other roommates?" he asked.

Luke shook his head. "Just the two of us. We live together in the home that we grew up in. It gives Jessica the space that she needs for all the animals that she brings home."

"That's convenient. It's nice seeing how close you two are to each other, and how you help her with the rescues."

"We're all we've got. Our parents died several years ago. Car accident."

"I'm sorry to hear that," Chance said. But Chance asked no more questions, so Luke didn't offer more information. It was a difficult subject that led to more difficult topics. When he saw they had both finished their soup, Luke stood, and headed back into the break room.

He returned with a pint of ice cream and two spoons. "And what about you, Doctor Chance? Do you have any siblings nearby?" he asked as he took off the lid and offered Chance the first taste.

"I do not. Only child," he said, and his eyes darkened at that. "I always wanted someone, anyone, to help take the spotlight off of me." He dug his spoon into the ice cream and tasted it. "Wow, this is amazing."

Luke was satisfied. "It is my favorite." But Chance's comment about the spotlight caught his attention. "Are you close to your parents?" he asked and took his own scoop from the creamy dessert.

Chance's face clouded over. "Yes and no. I see them every couple of weeks, and I love them. But we don't see eye-to-eye very often. Never, if I'm being honest, so all of our communication is superficial, surface-level small talk just to say we did."

Luke raised a single brow. "Do they live here?"

Chance nodded. "Sugarland," he said, naming a suburb of the city. "They love me, but they don't like me."

"I don't see how that's possible." Luke couldn't imagine anyone's parents being disappointed with the man sitting next to him. "I'm sorry, Doctor Chance, but that's ridiculous."

Chance soft smile spoke volumes. "Thanks for that show of support. But families can be tricky. I just didn't follow any of their plans for me, and constantly fail to live up to their expectations. I didn't go to the college of their choice, they didn't approve of vet school, I didn't marry the daughter of a family friend and give them three grandkids by the time I turned thirty." Chance cleared his throat. "And I'm gay, so there's that," he murmured, and dug his spoon in for more ice cream before handing it to Luke.

Luke nodded. "I'm so sorry." This conversation had become much deeper than he'd expected, and while it felt good opening up to this man, knowing about Chance's parents angered Luke. "Not that it matters, but I think you're amazing."

Chance handed the ice cream back to Luke with shining eyes. "Believe it or not, Luke, it matters a lot."

· · · · **·** · **·** · · ·

Luke's eyes blinked open. When had he fallen asleep? Where was he? And who covered him with a blanket?

A quick glance around the darkened room reminded him what happened—he was at the vet's office. He drifted off still sitting in a large rolling chair that he'd pushed near the cage with the injured dog he'd brought in. Luke had stayed to make sure she was okay—or if the worst happened, to ensure she didn't die alone.

He checked his phone for the time—a quarter after two in the morning. A sound at his left startled him. Doctor Chance, leaning back in his own chair, even more gorgeous as he slept. His head tilted to the side and his broad chest rose and fell with each deep breath.

For several minutes Luke refused to move, entranced. Being this close to a sleeping Chance was a literal dream come true. But his traitorous body had other ideas. A yawn escaped his mouth, so loud his jaw cracked.

Chance's eyes fluttered a few times as he woke and ran a hand through his hair. "Everything okay?" he asked as he sat up in his chair, his voice rough with sleep.

"I think so," Luke said and pointed at the cage. "Look at her." He stood and peered at the black lab. She was awake now, and her warm brown eyes were open, clear and curious. "You are feeling better, yes?" Luke asked and stuck his finger inside the crate so she could smell it. The dog leaned forward and pressed her face against it; she'd be okay, Luke knew this now. "Oh yes, you sweet girl."

Chance stood and stepped over to the light switch, then flicked it on, the room flooding with white light. He broke out into a smile when he saw her head bobbing up and down as Luke petted her. "Oh, she looks good." He walked to the crate and opened the door, then reached in and stroked her gently as he examined the wound. Her tail gave a soft thump, and he laughed. "Yes, she's feeling better too. The antibiotics kicked in, didn't they?" Chance turned back to Luke. "I think we're out of the woods. She's got a long road ahead, and we still might have to take that leg, but the medication and hydration have her on the right track."

A thousand emotions rushed through Luke. Elation, delight, that lingering fear that *maybe something still could go wrong* but Chance smiled, and that was enough for Luke, who stood next to Chance and snapped a quick picture of their recovering patient for Jessica. Then his eyes closed, and he grinned ear to ear, relief rushing through him. "That's amazing. Thank you." All the stress and worry they'd both experienced over this little black dog, it all seemed worth it right now. *She's going to be okay.* "You saved her life, Chance. You're incredible."

Luke hadn't meant those last two words to slip out.

But then Chance slid his arm around Luke's shoulder and gave him a squeeze as they stared at the dog. "*We* saved her life. She wouldn't be here without you, Luke."

The contact should have felt strange, awkward. Luke didn't let people close like this and yet—it was the most natural thing in the world, to lean against this tall, strong man, to feel the warmth of his body, even if it was just for a few seconds.

But it was also time to return to reality. "Okay, well, I suppose I'll go now. Can I call you tomorrow to see how she's doing?" Luke asked and slid his phone back into his pocket.

"Of course." Chance turned and faced Luke, with those over-bright blue eyes focused on him. This close, Luke made out the flecks of gold near the center, and those lips, full and pink and generous, they looked so soft.

And they were getting closer.

Luke froze.

What—

His eyes stayed open during that first unexpected kiss, just the barest brush of their lips, but his heart stopped beating entirely. That one soft kiss led to another, and this one deeper, and this time Luke's eyes closed as he surrendered to the sensation. Luke's hands reached out and found Chance's shirt, gripping the bottom hem. Chance lifted his hands and cradled Luke's face, lightest touches on his cheek, and he tugged at Luke's bottom lip with his own. But when the tip of Chance's tongue brushed against Luke's, it went bright, like fireworks behind his eyelids and it shook him out of this reverie. *This isn't happening.*

Luke stepped back automatically, still holding his breath. "Um—"

Chance stiffened and took a step back, his eyes wide with disbelief. "Oh God, I'm sorry—"

"No. Stop," Luke began, but Chance had already retreated away from him with a pained expression. "I didn't mean to—I don't—"

"Mr. Granger, I shouldn't have—"

Luke went numb. "No, it was okay. It surprised me, that's all. It wasn't that bad." *IT WASN'T THAT BAD?* Voices in Luke's head shrieked at him to stop talking, or to explain himself better, but every time he opened his mouth, it only made things worse. "It was a good kiss."

Chance's face reddened as he stared at the floor. "Thank you?" he said, confused.

"Yeah." Pressure built inside Luke's chest. It had all gone bad so quickly and now he needed to get away. "Okay, I better go then."

"I understand," Chance answered, and turned back to the dog's cage. He closed it and made a big deal out of checking her IV bag. "Someone will call in the morning about the dog." Then Chance turned back toward him, and they stared at each other for a long moment, neither man speaking. Eventually, Luke reached down into his pocket and felt for his keys and wallet.

Right where they belonged. "Um—good night," Luke said, and headed to the front of the clinic. He clumsily stumbled on a misplaced chair in the dark waiting room. Chance followed him and unlocked the front door and Luke pushed the door open, the tinkling door chime like laughter in his ears as he left the clinic without looking back.

Once he was back in his Subaru, it all hit him, the enormity of his fuck-up.

Classic Luke—*your wildest dream comes true, and you freak out.* He pounded the steering wheel a few times, his stomach knotted in dread. Why had he reacted like that? What did he say again— "It wasn't that bad."

He'll never want to see me again, and I can't blame him, he thought. Luke stared at the front door of the office for another minute before he turned on the car and headed home.

Chapter Eight

After Luke left, Chance situated the injured black lab, checked her medication, and made sure she was comfortable, then left detailed notes in her medical chart, describing how she'd progressed through the night. With that task completed, Chance headed upstairs for some sleep and tried to pretend that entire encounter had been in his imagination.

That Chance hadn't just kissed a client in a vulnerable moment of elation and relief.

His heart pounded in his chest as he pulled off his clothes and dropped them on the floor, the whole kiss still like a dream—or a nightmare, depending on Luke's reaction.

But it had happened.

Chance dropped heavily on his bed and glanced over at the bathroom as he yawned. A shower would feel good right now, he decided as he leaned back on the bed, and his head hit the pillow. *I hope Luke doesn't hate me.*

It was his last thought right before his eyes closed and he fell into a deep sleep.

Sunlight filled the room. Stretching, Chance rolled his head around his shoulders and blearily reached out for his phone. It was nearly noon, and he had three missed messages.

None of them were from Luke.

That's okay, nothing to panic about. Luke had probably done the same as him—gone home and slept after an extra-long day. But that kiss... All sorts of questions ran through Chance's head when he remembered the way Luke leaned into him, the rough scrape of stubble under Chance's fingertips. Maybe he hadn't been as distressed about it as Chance previously thought. Luke had kissed him back—and what a kiss—so clearly there had been *some* interest.

He pressed his fingers to his temple and squeezed. Should he make the first call? Or maybe he should wait for Luke to contact him to see if he was interested.

And what about the dog?

It had all happened so fast, and Chance wasn't even sure if Luke and his sister had lined up a foster for her when she was ready to head home.

Too many questions, but no answers would come from just sitting in bed all day. Chance sent a quick text to Dr. Berry and Norma downstairs, letting them know he was up and would be down within the hour.

Clara: *Sounds good. We'll see you then. I want to know more about this lab, her leg looks awful.*

Clara: *Does all this ice cream belong to you?*

She attached a photograph of the freezer in the breakroom, full of peach cobbler ice cream.

Chance stared at the photo. He'd forgotten about that, but it made him smile, the thought of Luke and his favorite flavor, and how they'd shared a pint after eating Chance's tortilla soup. It made Chance want to know more about him. The first man in years that Chance felt any attraction to, and he'd fucked it up by making a move at the worst possible moment, when Luke was tired, vulnerable, and emotional about the dog.

With any luck, Chance hadn't messed it all up.

Once Chance made it downstairs, he headed for the little black lab. "How she's doing?"

Clara Berry, his partner at the clinic, walked toward him in her matching blue scrubs. "She's a fighter, that's for sure. Norma showed me pictures from yesterday. Terrible wound." Clara's long dark hair was pulled back into a ponytail, a light sunburn on her cheeks. "She's a stray?"

she asked, and her hand slipped inside the cage and rested on the dog's soft fur.

"As far as I know. Luke said—" Chance stopped and cleared his throat. *We kissed right here.* "They found a bunch of them in a yard. She was the worst." Clara's eyes twinkled. Had Norma said something to her? "How was Hawaii?" he asked and changed the subject.

Her face lit up. "Wonderful. Crowded, but amazing. I'd love to go again, but not during the summer. Remind me I said that next time I plan a vacation."

"Will do."

Norma waited until after Dr. Berry left to interrogate him. "How long did he stay?" she asked as he held down a wriggling pug mix so she could clip his nails.

Here it goes. "I can't remember. Maybe two or three in the morning? I convinced him to go home eventually, and then I went upstairs around four." When Norma didn't move, he tilted his head at her. "You were expecting something else?" he asked and released the dog as she finished her task.

She smirked. "Maybe. I've always thought you two were cute together, and that one of these days... maybe something would happen," she said, and carried the pug back to exam room three, where her owner was waiting.

If only she knew.

· · · · ●·●·● · · ·

Drinking with friends on Thursday nights was harder now than it had been five years ago, especially when he'd been up super late last night with the injured dog, and then worked a full day. But Diego was a good friend, and his band was playing at Anarchy, a popular club. A few of their friends were heading out to support him and Chance had promised to go, so after he closed up the office, he took another quick shower after work and made sure Sheba had dinner, then headed out for a couple 'beers with the queers,' as Nolan liked to say.

Nolan was already there with his boyfriend, Harrison, and Diana, who was Diego's sister. They'd found a table in the back near the bar and waved Chance over once they spotted him. Diana patted the chair next to her. "Glad you could make it," she said, a broad smile on her face as she leaned over for a hug.

"I didn't want to miss this. They sound good!" Steel Horse always put on a great show, and had just put out their second album, which was getting some attention on Spotify. "I can't stay too long, but I wanted to hear the guys play. How's it been?" Chance asked and yawned behind his hand.

"So far so good," Nolan said with his usual cheeky grin, his shoulder-length dark hair pulled back off his face. "But the question is, how are you doing?" He waved at a passing server, and asked for another round for the table, including a beer for Chance. "It's not even eight-thirty, Doc." Nolan leaned against Harrison and kissed his cheek. "Even my old man here can stay up later than that."

Harrison was twenty years older than all of them, but when he smiled at Nolan's gentle tease, the age gap between them disappeared and all that remained was their clear love for each other. *Is that what it would be like to show Luke that sort of affection?* Chance shook his head and pushed those thoughts away. "I had a long night and didn't get much sleep."

Nolan's perfectly arched eyebrow raised so high it almost left his face. "Hopefully it was a good time."

Chance shrugged and assumed Nolan was teasing. His lack of a love life used to be a frequent topic of conversation among his circle of close friends, but as the years went by, they respected his privacy and stopped asking him about it. "Yes and no. I mean, I was at work. There was a dog who wasn't doing well." He talked louder to be heard over a particularly loud guitar riff. "I stayed downstairs at the clinic most of the night."

Diana smiled sympathetically. "Good for you. But couldn't you take a nap down there?"

The corners of Chance's lips turned up as he recalled the previous night. "Um, I wasn't alone. The guy who brought him in, he stayed with me." Three sets of eyes bore into him. "What?"

Nolan pointed a finger at him, his eyes wide with shock. "Your face. You got all dreamy. There's more to this than just the sick dog." He sat up and scooted his chair closer to Chance. "Who is this guy, and why did he stay?"

Dreamy? Chance's pulse raced, but he kept it cool on the outside. "The guy who brought the dog in—he wanted to be there in case he could help, or if things went bad. I guess he felt bad for the dog, didn't want her to be alone if she... didn't make it." Their faces dropped. "I didn't mean to bring everyone down. The dog's good now. She made it through the night, and now she's stable enough to be released to her foster family in the morning."

Diana clapped her hands. "Is it that same guy who brought her in?"

Chance nodded. "Him and his sister. They both take in the animals, and they live together."

"You know a lot about this guy," Nolan said. He sipped his drink.

Chance shrugged. "They bring in quite a few animals to the clinic."

"Do I know them?" Nolan asked. His mother worked with a local rescue organization, and he had several connections to that community through her.

"Um, I think your mom might know Jessica. Last name's Granger. They do local pickups and foster for the bigger groups." He thanked the waitress who stopped by their table and set down fresh drinks and cleared the empty glasses. He drank a quick swallow of his cold beer. "Her brother's name is Luke."

"And Luke wanted to stay with you last night." Nolan made an appraising noise. "Sounds like a nice guy."

Harrison took a drink from his beer, having watched this entire conversation with an amused expression. "Is he cute?" he asked.

Everyone at the table turned toward Harrison. "Look at you making assumptions, your honor," Nolan said, and touched Harrison's chest with a finger.

Harrison was a lawyer, so this must be one of their nicknames. But Harrison laughed. "One, examine the body language. Chance's crossed arms, the flush on his face. Normally he's got a bright sunshiny smile thing going on, but he got defensive when you brought up whatever happened last night. Second—he did look awfully dreamy there for a minute. The defense rests."

Nolan wrapped his arm around Harrison. "You know what that legal talk does to me, lover."

Diana coughed and Chance pushed his chair back from the table. "Get a room, guys."

Nolan kissed Harrison's cheek. "But really, are you okay? Harry's right—you look a little shell shocked."

How to explain what happened. "Okay. I guess I need to talk about it with someone." Chance took another long pull from his beer bottle. "I don't know exactly how it all went down, but we... kissed."

Their shocked faces made him smile. "Oh. I didn't expect that. Did you want to kiss him?" Diana asked.

It was a moment before Chance answered. "Yeah. Yeah, I did." Chance's hands curled around his beer. "The ladies at work, they've teased me about Luke for almost a year now, maybe longer. How I look at him when he comes in. How he looks at me." He pressed his lips together. "I don't know, I didn't intend on kissing him."

"So, you kissed first?" Nolan's voice dropped to a near whisper, impossible to hear in the bar.

But Chance knew what he asked and scratched the back of his head. "I think so. It happened so fast. We'd fallen asleep, and then he woke up first and woke me up to look at the dog. She was so much better than when they brought her in. Anyway, I told him she was going to make it, and he smiled, and we hugged and—" Chance took a breath before continuing. "He was right there, so close. So, I kissed him."

Diana sat frozen, entranced by this story, with her chin in her hands. "Did he kiss you back?"

Chance remembered that kiss—soft and sweet, then—*ohhh*. His face flushed red hot. "He did—but when it was over—" He shrugged and exhaled, waving one hand in front of him. "I don't know. We sort of pretended it didn't happen."

"What?" Nolan leaned forward, indignant. "You ignored it?"

Chance nodded. "Wrong move?"

Diana's shoulders slumped and Nolan hung his head. "Fuck yeah, wrong move, Sunshine. Now he's not going to think that you like him." Nolan tapped Harrison's shoulder. "Harry, honey, back me up here."

Harrison's gaze was warm and friendly, but Chance knew he genuinely cared about him and all of Nolan's friends, and that he'd offer rock-solid advice. "Do you want a relationship with Luke?"

That was the question. "I think so. But I'm sure Nolan's told you—I don't date often."

Nolan snorted. "You don't date ever. It's bizarre."

Chance took a deep breath and exhaled slow. "I've had some unpleasant experiences in the past, and all that taught me is that getting close to other people is generally not worth it. I've got family issues to think about, and my time is limited as it is." But all of those were excuses. "Truth is, I just don't feel like I have much to offer someone."

Diana punched Chance's shoulder. "That's insane. You're smart, kind, you have an amazing job, and you're crazy good-looking. I'm serious, Chance. You look like a movie star. Easily the hottest guy in this bar right now—sorry fellas," Diana said to Nolan, who looked put out, and Harrison, who grinned.

"That's sweet of you to say." But hadn't that been part of the problem too? Boys chasing him for his looks, not caring about the heart and soul underneath his blond hair and blue eyes. "Have I fucked it up royally with this guy?"

That would be rich. The first man Chance wanted to date in years, and he screwed it up before it began.

"What was the last thing you said to him?" Harrison asked.

"Um, I told him that someone would call him or his sister about the dog in the morning. Then I said good night. No good-night kiss," Chance added quickly when he saw Diana open her mouth to ask.

Nolan frowned. "Not the most auspicious beginning—did you like how I used that word? Me and big words, you're impressed, I know. You fucked up your first kiss, but that doesn't mean you're going to fuck up number two. Where's the dog right now?"

"Jessica came to get her this afternoon and took her back to their house. She'll rehab better there, less noise and activity than at the clinic." The three of them looked at each other, then back at Chance. "What? Am I missing something?"

Nolan's shoulders fell. "Beautiful, but dumb. Fucking tragic. How about you go over to his house tomorrow after work and check on the dog? A house call, so to speak."

Diana's head bobbed up and down. "And while you're there, you can feel out what his feelings toward you are. Do you think he likes you?"

Chance nodded and smiled. "I think so, despite how badly it all turned out last night."

"Then go find out. And ask him on a proper date." Nolan leaned back and tucked himself against Harrison's side.

Just then, Diego appeared at their table, his long dark hair shiny with sweat. They'd been so wrapped up in their conversation, no one noticed that the music ended. "What did you think?" he asked as he dropped into an empty chair.

"What did we think about what?" Diana asked.

Diego's eyes narrowed. "That last song. It's off the new album, the one that Javier and I wrote. Troy mentioned that before we began playing." Dark eyes bore into each of them. "What was so interesting that none of you paid any attention to our new song?" he asked as he accepted the bottle of water from his sister.

All eyes turned toward Chance again. *Nope, not right now.* "I'll tell you later, D," he said, as Troy, the band's guitarist and Harrison's son, joined them, and Harrison handed him a fresh beer.

Chapter Nine

After spending the night at the clinic, Luke had slept until eleven; unheard of for him, even with his typically late hours playing games with his friends online. But even after his eyes opened, he lingered in bed, his legs twisted in his sheets, as he ran through the events of the previous night.

He kissed Chance. Or had Chance kissed him?

Luke had never reacted like that to a kiss, even his first one, back as an awkward teenager who knew even less about flirting. There had been a few men who he'd intimately known, and while he rarely slept over at their houses or invited them to sleep at his, he enjoyed the sexual act itself.

But relationships took up time and energy and invited people inside your bubble on a long-term basis. That part is where Luke often failed, maintaining those personal connections, until one day he'd wake up and realize his lovers left him behind for greener and more interested pastures.

Luke pulled his pillow over his head. Did it matter? All Luke knew was that he'd frozen in place and Chance had apologized as if he'd done something wrong. *Should he call him?* And what would Luke say? That he didn't mind being kissed? That he'd wanted to kiss Chance for months? That their kiss was the best thing to happen to him in a very, very long time?

Would it even do any good? It was unlikely that Chance would believe him, not after Luke's erratic behavior.

How would they ever get past this debacle?

A sound from his phone caught his attention. For the briefest of moments, Luke thought it might be from Chance.

> Jess: *I'm running errands and then going to get the dog from the clinic before I head home. You want me to bring you a burger?*

> Luke: *Yes, plain and dry with tots.*

> Jess: *ffs*
> Jess: *I'll just get you a toddler meal.*

He also noticed some direct messages sent to him from his gamer group's Discord channel, so Luke reached over and flipped his computer on. After a quick shower, where he tried and failed not to jack himself off, Luke threw on an old t-shirt and cargo shorts and sat down in front of the computer.

Pecos Bob: *I thought we were on for Planet Zombie last night. You bailed on us, L.*

Grungy: *I told you guys, an emergency came up. But we can do an afternoon session if you want.*

Pecos Bob: *What kind of emergency? Your sis?*

Nicknack Padywack: *I can't remember the last time you stayed at someone else's house*

Grungy: *Wasn't at a house. Was at the vet with a dog.*

Nicknack Padywack: *The cute vet?*

Was there anyone who didn't know about Luke's crush on Chance? Granted, Nick, who Luke met from Jessica's rescue work, might have met Chance through their rescue connections.

How many people knew Chance as 'that cute vet'?

Grungy: *Are we playing or not? I'm free all day.*

Pecos Bob: *Light em up.*

Nicknack Padywack: *cool cool you guys mind if I stream this?*

After a couple hours of playing, Luke looked out his window and Jessica's Explorer was pulling up into their driveway.

Grungy: *Gimme ten. BRB.*

Luke jogged downstairs and opened the front door. "How's she doing?" he asked and took the crate from Jessica's hands.

Jessica's shoulders rose and fell. "Thanks. She's good. Her leg still looks awful, but they think they got the infection under control. Most of the redness and swelling is gone, but we need to restrict activity as much as possible, and she shouldn't put any weight on that leg until she goes in for her check-up next week. But the good news is Doctor Clara thinks there's a chance she'll be able to use it again. She said you and Doctor Chance did a great job with her yesterday."

Luke ignored that comment because it hurt. "Where do you want her?" he asked as he carried the dog into the house. Her tail thumped twice at the sound of his voice. "Oh, they put you in a cone, my poor girl."

Jessica laughed. "Yeah, she'll have that on for a while, until that wound heals. Can you put her in the back room? I'm keeping Betsy, Junebug, and Ginger upstairs until we figure out logistics."

Luke settled the recovering lab in the room Jessica used when she needed to isolate or quarantine her dogs, while Jessica ran back out to her car and returned with their lunch and Luke's insulated grocery bag. "Thanks again for coming so fast yesterday. Maggie's got the other two dogs and the puppies, at least for a few days. I told her I'd keep our sweet girl here." She put their food on the kitchen table and set the insulated bag on the counter. "Everyone at the clinic said they wanted to try this ice cream but didn't want you to get mad at them, so they left it alone." Jessica opened the freezer and filled it with Luke's ice cream and frozen dinners. "Those ladies think you're pretty special."

"Special?" Luke said and touched his head.

Jessica narrowed her eyes at him. "They're very fond of you, warts and all. Norma said you staying with Doctor Chance to make sure Sadie was okay really impressed them. She said that you helped them out when they worked on her."

"I just—" He'd stood there, passed them things they needed and tried not to get in their way. "I've got to get back upstairs. Thank you for lunch and for bringing my frozen goods."

Luke grabbed his bag of fast food and headed out of the kitchen. Jessica caught him and hugged him tight.

"Jess," he began, but she shushed him.

"I think you're special too, Luke." She kissed his cheek and swatted his shoulder. "Don't stay up there all day. You need some sunshine."

Sunshine. The word reminded him of Chance's smile, his eyes, his hair. Yes, Luke wanted that kind of sunshine, maybe even needed it.

But he'd messed it up.

Luke paused at the door, comprehending something Jess said earlier. "Sadie?" he asked.

Jessica nodded and popped a fry into her mouth. "It's cute, isn't it? She looks like a Sadie to me."

"I like it. You did good with her, too, Jessica." Luke returned his sister's bright smile and headed up to his room for an afternoon of shooting zombies and reclaiming planets.

Chapter Ten

The clinic's schedule was light for a Friday, and Chance spent time in the office working on patient charts earlier than normal. "I might have these knocked out before closing time," he said to Norma as she tidied up the supply closet.

"Good news. Maybe you can go out and have some fun with your friends again." She'd been glad to hear that he'd gone out the night before.

Lazlo—cat, male tabby. Chance finished inputting his surgical notes in the computer file, then flipped over the paper record and stared a moment at the next folder in the pile. *Stray (Luke Granger)—dog, female black lab.* Just seeing his name had Chance's heart beating faster, and he glanced over to that spot in the back room where they'd kissed.

This was exactly the problem Chance had expected. His job was to tend to the animal's health and welfare, and upon seeing the animal's name, his initial thoughts had all been about his desire for the man who brought her in. Unprofessional.

The dog's care was the most important thing. In most circumstances, when they released an animal with that level of injury back to their family, either he or Clara called in that evening to check on how their pet was progressing. But right now, Chance's thoughts were on that kiss, the way Luke leaned into him, then pulled back, shocked.

Stray (Luke Granger)—dog, female black lab. Chance's hand reached for the phone. Despite those feelings, Chance needed information about the dog, and to find out how she was doing at their home.

That's all, right?

But before he dialed, Nolan's words swam through his head. *Make a house call, idiot.*

He glanced at the clock on the wall. It was nearly closing time.

Thirty minutes later, Chance sat in his Chevy Tahoe, still in his scrubs, and stared at the navigation app at his phone, where he'd typed in the Granger's address, retrieved from the computer files.

This was stupid. At the very least, he should call first. But something inside Chance's head worried that if he called, Luke would tell him the dog was okay and that he didn't need to come over. Was he being selfish, wanting to see him? Wanting to hear from the man's own mouth that he didn't want to go out with him? That Luke didn't want more of those soft, sweet kisses?

Chance was surprised as he pulled into their suburban neighborhood, filled with older houses, most of them with two stories and big lawns with mature trees. Despite what Luke had told him that night that they talked and shared with each other, it wasn't what he'd expected from two young people in their twenties. Parking in front of their house, Chance double-checked the address before he walked to the front door and rang the doorbell.

A minute later, Luke answered the door in a t-shirt and shorts. He looked shocked to see him. "Hi, Doctor Chance."

"Hi there." Chance's voice wavered as he spoke. "I wanted to check in and see how she was doing. The dog, I mean. She got discharged while I was with a patient, and I didn't get to say goodbye. I—" Suddenly, the enormity of what Chance had done hit him. He'd just driven over here and ambushed this poor man who clearly didn't want this attention from Chance (or he would have called, right?) "Um, I'm sorry. I guess I should've called and asked if it was okay to come over."

But Luke shook his head, soft brown curls bouncing. "It's fine. Come in." He opened the door wide for Chance to enter.

His first thought was that the interior space was roomy, like a big family home, but not much had changed in a couple of decades. The furniture and decor were clean and neat but dated. Luke told him he and his sister grew up in that house, and now that he saw it, he understood better. They'd been children here, and that small detail tugged on Chance's heartstrings. "How are you doing? I hope I didn't bother you."

Luke shook his head again and walked Chance toward a room in the back of the house. "I was tinkering with some code. Debugging," he said with a shrug. They walked into what might've once been a playroom or den, but now held dog crates and dog beds, water bowls and chew toys. "We've got her over here resting," Luke said, and knelt next to a large crate with a sleeping dog inside.

Chance bent down to see her and was gratified when those soft brown eyes perked up as he approached. "Eating and drinking?" he asked as he opened the cage, then reached inside to pet her head.

"We've given her a small meal and offered water every few hours. Jessica cleaned the wound this morning and afternoon the way Dr. Berry showed her. Do you want to see it?"

"In a moment." Chance reached into his pocket and pulled out a penlight and shone it into her eyes. "Have you named her yet?"

Luke's head tilted to the side as he reached in and touched a paw. "Jessica's calling her Sadie."

Sadie. "I love it. And it suits her." Chance settled on the ground and opened the cage. "Come here, Sadie." Carefully, he lifted her out of the crate so he could look at her, pleased to see her trying to get up on her own. "Easy girl, not so fast." Chance smiled at Sadie's eagerness to stand. "Jessica did a great job with the bandage."

"I'll let her know." Luke sat down next to Chance as he looked over at the dog. "Doctor Chance, I wanted to thank you for taking such loving care of her when we came in. I know you don't usually camp out downstairs with patients like that."

He blinked. "Oh, I'm glad you brought her to me. It was an honor to work on such a sweet girl and be part of her recovery." Chance scratched Sadie behind her ears, and that small tail wag of hers spoke volumes; she was on her way to recovery. "And I wanted to thank you for staying with me. Talking to you, and you listening to me—it meant a lot. It's not easy for me to talk about my family sometimes, and you were a patient listener." Luke flushed at that compliment, so Chance pushed a little further. "And I hope you weren't upset when I kissed you. I apologize for that."

"Upset?" Luke's eyes went wide as saucers. "Why would that upset me?"

Had he been holding his breath that whole time? Must've been because Chance let it all go when Luke looked at him like that. "I—I wasn't sure. You left, and we didn't talk, or kiss again, or—" *Smooth, Chance.* He closed his eyes and collected his thoughts. *Get this right.* "I'm glad you were there, Luke, and I'm glad we kissed. I'd like to hang out with you more, away from the office."

Luke's hands laced together in front of him, and Chance didn't know if he felt better or worse at how nervous Luke seemed. "Are you asking me out on a date?" he asked, his face inscrutable.

Chance hoped he'd read the situation right. "Yes, like a date. Do you want to have dinner with me, or maybe go see a movie?"

Luke nodded, small movements at first, but his eyes lit up and his smile took Chance's breath away. "I would enjoy that."

"Oh good." Sadie looked back and forth at them, as if she'd been following the conversation. "Okay, good." Chance rubbed Sadie's ears and grinned at her expressive eyes. "She's going to be a happy girl once we've got her all healed up." Chance glanced around the room. "No other fosters with you guys right now?"

Luke snorted. "There are always dogs here, Doctor Chance. Currently, we are hosting a poodle mix and a golden retriever as well as Miss Junebug—you remember her. Jessica's keeping them out of this room while Sadie heals." Luke pointed at the window. "She's out walking them, working on their leash training."

One more scratch behind the ears for Sadie, and Chance gently got her back into her crate. "She can start spending more time out of the crate, as long as someone's around to watch her. Hopefully those leg muscles will heal, and she'll be able to use that leg again."

"I will relay the message to Jess." They stood, and Luke walked him toward the front door. "I'd ask if you could stay for a while, but I need to finish this debugging project tonight, if I can."

"No, it's cool." Chance pictured what Sheba's face would look like if he was any later getting home. "I've got to go too. But maybe we can hang out tomorrow night?"

Luke nodded, his face serious, but those hazel eyes—they shone bright. "Call me later, if you've got time."

"I will." One more glance at each other, and Chance headed toward his Tahoe. As he opened the driver's side door, he pumped his fist in victory.

Chapter Eleven

An exasperated noise came from the doorway to Luke's room. "Do you want to go shopping?"

Luke's brows furrowed deep. He stood outside his closet and reached for a dark blue plaid shirt. He gave it a quick sniff before he turned toward Jessica. "Why? My clothes are acceptable." Jessica's eyes rolled to the back of her head. "Your face will get stuck like that one of these days."

The insult did not stop her from barging into his room. "You have, like, three shirts that aren't t-shirts, and even those are just plaid and flannel."

She wasn't wrong. "They're comfortable and serviceable."

Jessica laughed. "But they're not sexy. Don't you want to look nice for your veterinarian boyfriend?"

Now it was Luke's turn to scoff. "He's hardly—"

"Luke." Jessica stepped close to her brother, and her hands cupped his face with warm familiarity, like Chance had done to him a few days before. "Cut this self-abasement shit out. I know you like this guy, and there is nothing wrong with that. Let's go get you something nice to wear tonight." She kissed his forehead. "Besides, I thought gay guys were supposed to like shopping."

"Clearly that's not the case," Luke said quietly, but he nodded after another glance in his closet. "For the record, I don't think Chance cares what I wear tonight. My flannel shirts never bothered him before."

She tickled the back of his hair. "That's because he was curious about what's underneath." Luke's face froze with mock outrage as Jessica cackled. "C'mon. I've been dying to give you a makeover for years."

They walked through the men's department of Macy's, weaving in and out of the various racks of summer clothing. "Do you know where you're going tonight?" she called out as he tried on some pants.

Luke stepped out of the fitting room and handed her a pair of khakis with an affirmative nod, both to the question and the khakis. "I'm meeting him at Blue Hen. It is a farm-to-market sort of experience, and fairly popular right now." Luke had gleaned that from their website when he checked out their menu to make sure there was something he'd enjoy. "Then we may go see a movie afterward, if we feel like it and find something we both enjoy." He'd been excited at first when Chance wanted to take him somewhere nice. But the later in the day it got, the more Luke started to worry.

But Jessica just beamed. "Classic first date. What kind of movie?"

Luke shrugged. "That has not yet been decided."

"Are you nervous?" Jessica asked. She handed him a pair of fitted jeans.

He handed them back to her with a shake of his head. "No. A little." Luke's face remained impassive, but his voice dropped, hard to hear. "You know I don't enjoy large crowds."

Jessica leaned in close. "I know, Luke. But this guy, he's special, isn't he?"

Luke nodded. "He thinks I'm funny—and not funny because I am—" Luke's hands waved in front of his face. "I realize there is something off about my personality. A distinct lack of charm in my genetics."

Jessica caught his hand. "You're a great guy, Luke. And there's nothing wrong with your genetics. A little quirky, but there are several of us who appreciate your wacky side." She pushed the jeans back into his hands.

Luke stopped walking. His shoulders slumped at the idea of wearing these tight jeans. "I have never been called wacky a day in my life."

"Not to your face." Her arm wrapped around his shoulder. "Come this way." She led him to a rack of long-sleeved shirts. "I think a crisp white shirt would be nice. You can roll up the sleeves and wear it with some jeans or khakis." She pushed through several until she found one in his size. "You're going to look simply smashing tonight."

He accepted the shirt without complaint. "Aunt Linda will be happy to hear I went out."

Jessica growled softly and picked through another rack of shirts. "She's a nosy busybody. The less she knows, the better."

"She's the only family we have left." Luke nudged Jessica with his elbow until she turned and faced him. "I believe she wants what is best for us. She worries about you." When Jess didn't meet his eyes, he placed his hand on her shoulder. "I worry about you as well."

That stopped her. She gazed up at Luke. "I know how to take care of myself."

"I do not doubt that," Luke said, even though he harbored many doubts. "But I wish you would not put yourself in those situations in the first place."

Jessica turned back to the clothing racks. "Someone has to look after them, to be their voice. Those innocent dogs are out there, hurting and abandoned. No one else is doing this, Luke. I have to help if I can."

"I know." This was a passionate mission for Jessica, almost a religious calling. How did one argue with that? Luke accepted the dark gray Henley shirt she handed him without protest. "Just be safe. Please."

"Always." But Jessica's eyes didn't meet Luke's as they walked toward the front of the store to ring up his purchases.

Chapter Twelve

Chance looked down at his supply list and laughed. Despite Gigi's youth and vivaciousness, she had the handwriting of an old lady, and her antiquated penmanship amused him.

Eight boxes of gloves, four large bottles of disinfecting cleaner, two large hand sanitizer refills, six clear plastic tarps, four packages of paper towels, zip ties (at least four inches long), four boxes of trash bags—both the tall, white ones and large green lawn bag.

The home improvement store located a few miles down the road had most of the cleaning supplies that the clinic needed, but Chance couldn't find the zip ties. He pushed his heavy shopping cart up one aisle and down the next and looked for someone in a red smock to help him out.

But as he turned the corner, someone called his name. "Hey Chance!"

It was Noah Reynolds, standing next to the paint counter. "Hey, what's up?" Chance asked and rolled his cart closer to Noah. "It's good to see you." Some twins were hard to tell apart, but Noah and Nolan Reynolds had such distinctive personalities that it was impossible to mix them up, even if Noah didn't keep his dark hair short and wear wire-rimmed glasses. A quick glance down into Noah's cart answered Chance's question—paint brushes, blue painter's tape, and a couple of tarps. "Painting project?"

Noah nodded and pointed at the employees on the other side of the counter, mixing up paint cans for the small line of waiting customers. "Yep. I finally decided to spruce up my bedroom. Since it's the one room in my money pit of a house that doesn't need any major renovation, I hoped that maybe a new color would help make it look less shitty."

Chance laughed at his pessimistic friend. "Shut up. You love that shitty house of yours."

Noah growled low. "I thought I did. Did you hear about my kitchen?" Noah pushed his glasses higher up on his nose and exhaled loud. "The contractor flaked out on me, the one that was supposed to put up the new cabinets. Just fucked off with my deposit, and not a word."

Shit. "No, I hadn't heard. I'm sorry, man." Chance had experienced a little of what renovations were like when his studio was being installed, but since he hadn't lived there during the construction, it hadn't been much of an inconvenience. "Can you get any of your money back?"

"I hope. Nolan said Harrison can file something for me. I don't know. Perks of having a lawyer in the family." Noah shrugged. "We'll see, I guess. At any rate, I thought that maybe if my bedroom wasn't completely fucked, it would be a nice place to relax and spend time, so I bought a new bedspread and some fake plants." He tapped the paint swatch. "What do you think?" he asked and held up a swatch of dark gray.

Stormy Night Out. Chance laughed. "That's a bold choice for a bedroom. You don't think it's a bit—dark?"

Noah nodded with a deep sigh. "Yeah, maybe picking out your paint color when you're mad isn't the smartest choice, but here we are." Now Noah looked down into Chance's cart and saw the cleaning supplies. "For the clinic, I hope. Otherwise, I've got some serious questions to ask."

Chance laughed. "Yep, it's all for work. We really should just have these delivered, but our needs are so different from week to week. And I don't mind making the trip out here every couple of weeks or so."

"That makes sense. Well, have you got any special plans tonight? If you want to help a poor grad student fix up his house and improve his mental health, I'll buy pizza and beer," Noah offered. "It's been a while since we hung out, just the two of us."

Chance shook his head. "I can't, not tonight. I've got a—" *Wait.*

Noah furrowed his brows when Chance stopped talking. "Hold on. You're going out on a date?" he asked, his voice dropping comically low, much like his twin did when they heard startling news.

"I—yes, I have a date tonight." Chance noticed that Noah's reaction was the opposite of Nolan's. Not grinning or clapping his hands, but thoughtful and serious. The twins could be so similar at times. They used the same facial expressions and had the same pauses in their speech, the way they inflected certain words. But other times, they were like night and day. Chance liked Noah, and even though Noah had none of Nolan's peppy effervescence, Noah called it like he saw it and didn't hold back his opinions, even if they weren't popular. He always offered measured, solid advice, and understood better than any of his friends what this meant to Chance, going out on a date after such a long hiatus. "What do you think?"

Noah blinked. "I think it's about time." He leaned against the paint counter. "When was your last first date?"

Chance leaned against the counter as well, mirroring Noah's stance. "Every January, I log into one of those dating sites and talk to someone for a few days. We go out twice, and—" He shook his head. "It just isn't what I want. I spend the entire time wishing I was at home." It struck Chance that he hadn't done that this past January. "It's been at least a year since I went out with someone, and nearly five since I dated anyone seriously." *Five years.*

Saying it out loud shook Chance. "You think there's something wrong with me?"

Noah frowned. "No, of course not. Some people aren't into dating and sex without feeling that emotional connection. But I am super curious about what changed, and why you've broken your 'no dating' rule."

Was it a rule? "Um, what changed?" Chance repeated. "I guess—I just really like this guy. And we met naturally, in real life. I wasn't just a few pictures he swiped right on. I think he likes me for more than just a good time."

"So, this isn't a one-night stand sort of date. Not a 'hit it and get it'?" Noah asked.

"Absolutely not," Chance answered. "Luke, he's a special kind of guy. You know, I almost had to convince him to go out with me."

Noah barked a laugh. "Damn, when was the last time that ever happened to you, Mister Movie Star?"

"I don't think that's ever happened," Chance said and laughed because Noah understood. This wasn't Chance being boastful. This meant that Luke didn't want a quick fuck with a hot guy. "Wish me luck tonight."

Noah snorted. "You don't need luck. You just need to show up and smile pretty and be charming and smart and whatever. Me, I'm the one that needs luck. Wish me luck that I don't paint my bedroom this fucking almost black color and then regret it in the morning." A clerk behind the counter waved at Noah and held up two cans of paint.

"Guess we'll see," Noah sighed, and reached for one of the cans.

Chance picked up the other can and set it carefully inside Noah's shopping cart next to the other one. "Send me a picture, will you? I'm dying to see how it turns out."

"If I don't hate it, maybe we can have a cookout soon at my place. I'll pick up some ribs and some lumber, and everyone can help me build a new deck out back while the meat cooks."

"You're on," Chance said, and wondered what it would be like to introduce Luke to his friends. It was a nice thought and put a smile on his face as he headed back to look for his zip ties.

Chapter Thirteen

That evening, Luke double-checked his hair in the hallway mirror. Touching his pockets, he felt his wallet, phone, and keys. Chance had texted the address earlier that day, and they'd agreed to meet at seven.

Luke's map app on his phone indicated the drive would be twenty-six minutes. His heart raced as he reached for the front door. No need to be nervous. It was just a date, Luke reminded himself, as if he went on dates all the time.

And yet, he couldn't help the optimistic smile on his face as he closed the door behind him.

Twenty-six minutes later, Luke pulled into Blue Hen and found a parking spot close to the front. The red brick restaurant appeared to be quite popular, as he spotted a long line of patrons waiting for their tables.

Chance stood near the entrance to the restaurant and waved him over. "Hi," he said, and walked toward Luke. "I called ahead and made reservations, so they're getting our table ready right now."

Chance wore a black long-sleeve shirt, pushed up to his elbows, and dark jeans. Luke's eyes went wide at the sight of the man in front of him. "You're not wearing scrubs." After all his concern about shopping, it never occurred to him that Chance might dress up as well. "You look nice."

Chance laughed. "I take them off sometimes, yeah. You look great too."

Luke looked at his shirt, touching the crisp fabric. "Jess picked it out."

"Jess did good." Chance's phone vibrated, and they both glanced down at it. "Our table's ready."

Luke followed Chance as they headed toward their table. It wasn't his imagination—there really were people looking at Chance, this beautiful man who looked even more amazing tonight. Luke's heart raced just being close to him, but the thought of other people seeing them together had his nerves on edge.

But once they settled into their seats, Luke forgot about the movie star looks and fell under the spell of Chance's warm personality. "How's our girl?" Chance asked, as he thanked the server who brought a basket of fresh bread to their table.

"She's doing well. Jess took her outside a few times to let her urinate, without putting any weight on the leg, and both times were successful." Luke reached for one soft loaf and tore it in two, absently handing half to Chance, who took it with a grin. "Jessica posted video from her rescue online, and now several people have contacted her regarding fostering her during her rehabilitation and possible adoption when she's ready."

"I'm not surprised. She's a special girl, and I mean, I saw the video. It was a terrible environment you guys took her from." Chance's face went pink, an unusual look on him. "I saw you there, too. You carried her away from that place."

It was Luke's turn to flush. "I just did what Jessica told me to do." Had he even noticed anyone filming him? "She really was in such bad shape."

"But you saved her." A waiter dressed in all black arrived at their table and took their orders—roast chicken and root vegetables for Chance and short ribs with garlic mashed potatoes for Luke. "Will she be heading to a new foster home soon?" Chance asked.

"Probably." Luke's eyes dropped. That would be a sad day for him. "But she has stabilized, and ultimately it would be better for her to be with someone who has no other dogs around, at least right now, so she can heal. It can be difficult keeping her separated from Jessica's other rescues."

Chance caught that look on Luke's face. "But you'll miss her."

"She is a sweet dog." Many of them were, but they cycled quickly through Jessica's rescue organization. It didn't make sense for Luke to get too attached. "I am certain that part of the foster agreement with be that Sadie remains under your care, for at least the first several months."

"I hope so."

Their food arrived, and both men tucked into it. "I was curious about your house," Chance said. "I know the other night you mentioned that you had grown up there, but I guess—" Chance took a deep breath. "It seems so big for just you and your sister. No one else lives there with you?"

Luke had an idea what Chance was asking. "It is a lot of house, at least it was at first." Those dark days after the accident had been rough, when Luke and Jessica made their stand to stay put and wait it out, despite pressure from others to move somewhere smaller. Luke folded his hands in front of him. "I told you that our parents died in a car accident eight years ago. The house belongs to my sister and me, but it's held in a trust. In three years, the deed transfers to me, and then Jessica and I will decide what we want to do with it."

"I'm so sorry about your parents," Chance said. "Was your family close?"

"Very close," Luke said. Was it time for 'the talk'? Luke cleared his throat and set his fork down. "Um—me, the way I am. It used to be worse, believe it or not, and I occasionally had trouble at school. But my parents made sure that I received whatever support I needed. My mother, in particular, she was very determined to help me learn how to... *interact* with the world around me." Luke fell silent and remembered some of the more vocal parent conferences with teachers. "Any success I have achieved is due to her, to both of them."

"She sounds like a special person." Chance tilted his head, as if he could see Luke better. "When you say that way you are, do you mean—"

"The autism spectrum? Yes, that's the official terminology, though Jessica prefers to use the word 'quirky' when she talks about it. High functioning, but quirky." Luke's fingers made air quotes when he said that word, but inside he quivered. "Does that bother you?" he asked, nervous about Chance's reaction.

But Chance shook his head. "No, of course not. I just want to know all about you—*quirks* and all."

Luke laughed at that, his heart fluttering inside. He picked up his fork and began eating again. "I'm glad. Anyway, when my parents made their wills, Jessica and I were still children, and they placed everything in this trust. I imagine they weren't sure how I was going to turn out, being—quirky." Luke coughed. "Then they passed away and my aunt, who is the executor, checks in with us to make sure we're behaving."

"But you don't have to live there."

Luke smiled wryly. "And yet, we're still there. A psychiatrist's dream, I imagine, peeking into our subconsciousness to figure that puzzle out."

Chance shook his head. "I don't think it's that difficult. It's a happy place for you, full of good memories."

"Also, no rent," Luke added.

Chance tossed his head back and laughed. "There's that."

Luke took another bite of his excellent food. "These short ribs are amazing." But he wanted to continue this conversation about them and learn more about Chance. "Did you have a happy childhood?" Chance had mentioned a rocky relationship with his mother. "Did you grow up close by?" Luke asked.

Chance nodded. "Yeah, Houston born and bred. But when I was little, I spent a lot of time with my grandparents. Nanna—that's what we all call her—she still lives in Galveston, in a big house close to the water. I grew up knowing that my grandparents were these super rich, fancy people, but to me, they were just my Nanna and Papa."

"That sounds amazing." Luke had few memories of any extended family, and other than their Aunt Linda, he and Jessica were alone. "So, when you say 'super rich,' do you mean—"

"Oh." Chance's lips curled into a small smile. "Sometimes I forget there might be people who don't automatically know about my family. My full name is Donovan

Chance Edwards IV. I guess if we're dating, you should know that."

Luke's eyes widened. "So your grandfather—no, great-grandfather," Luke said, doing the math in his head. "Dandy Don Edwards. He was the wildcat who discovered oil fields in East Texas and made millions." A Texas legend, so famous even Luke was familiar with the story. "Then your family owns a lot of oil refineries."

Chance nodded as he chewed. "We manage them. Somewhere along the line, most of them got sold to the Saudis for—for a ridiculous amount of money. More money than any person would know what to do with. My grandparents established a charitable foundation, and that's what I'm most proud of. They were great people, and they loved having all of us grandkids around their beach house. Unconditional love, no matter what we did."

Out of everything that Chance had just said, it was the mention of his grandparents that made Luke smile. "That sounds like a fun place to grow up."

Chance smiled at those memories. "It really was. In retrospect, I think my parents wanted me to be the favorite grandchild, so they let me hang out with Nanna and Papa as much as possible. But they loved me very much, and it was my favorite place in the whole world." He finished his drink. "I never felt that in my own childhood home."

Luke listed in rapt attention, still in shock that anyone could be disappointed in Chance. "Isn't it strange, how my parents accepted me despite my faults, but I don't have them anymore, while you have parents that can't accept their perfect son?"

"Whoa, wait. I'm not perfect." Chance reached out and rested his hand on Luke's. "And your 'quirks,' they're not faults. They're part of you, and I think you're amazing."

Luke's face went hot, but he flipped his hand, and let their fingers lace together for a moment. "Thank you," he said, pulling away just as someone came and bussed their table.

Chance leaned back in his chair. "I know we did it backwards, having out first date after our first kiss, but I think it's gone well so far."

Luke barked out a laugh, loud enough for the nearby tables to notice. "I agree."

"Did you feel like seeing a movie tonight?" Chance pulled out his phone. "There's that new one with Adam Driver. It's supposed to be good. Or that newish one about the superheroes if that's more your jam." Then Chance frowned. "Or... maybe not?"

Luke looked up. Had he made some sort of face at Chance's suggestion? "Both of those movies sound great. But I just—" It was hard to explain, especially to 'new' people. "I prefer not to be around large crowds."

"Oh." Chance had that look on his face, the one that Luke recognized. Confusion and pity and wariness, as people tried to diagnose what was wrong with him. "Oh, okay then."

Well, that was good while it lasted. "I'm sorry for messing up your plans for tonight."

"Mess up? No way." Chance took a breath, his eyes locked on his phone as he scrolled and tapped on the screen. "Just means it's time to be creative." Then it happened again, the million-dollar smile. "Got it. Movie with no crowds. You still game?" he asked, eyes dancing.

That smile was infectious, and right now Luke would've followed Chance into an arena filled with thousands of people, just to see that smile aimed at him again. "Yes."

But then Chance showed him his phone, with two tickets purchased for a local drive-in movie theater. Luke's stomach flipped pleasantly, knowing that he'd never have to do anything drastic like that for Chance.

Chance understood him.

Chance paid the check, despite Luke's protests. "I asked you out first. You can get the popcorn and drinks later," he said as they walked outside the restaurant and toward the parking lot. "Do you want to ride with me over there, and then I'll bring you back here? Or should we go to your house and drop off your car, and we can go from there together? It's not too far from where you live."

It would take longer for Chance to bring him back to the restaurant afterward and then drive home, so Luke agreed to drive back to his house and leave his car. Traffic was light and Luke would have to re-listen to that chapter in his audiobook as he drove, because he heard none of it. All his thoughts were Chance, and how good that conversation at dinner had gone.

When Luke parked in his driveway, Jessica's car was parked in front, so he sent her a quick text to let her know what was going on, and then jumped into Chance's Tahoe as it pulled up behind him.

They got to the drive-in theater and Chance backed his Tahoe into a parking spot. "I'm glad it's not too hot tonight," he said as he got out of his side and walked to the vehicle's rear. He opened the hatchback and lowered the back seats, creating a space for them to sit in relative privacy while being able to watch the movie. "I think we can hear on our phones, if you want to—" Chance pointed at a sign with an FM frequency.

Luke looked around, still amazed at Chance's idea. "This theater has been here for years, and yet I don't believe I have ever been here."

Chance laughed. "Me neither, though there was one in Galveston when I was a kid, and we all used to go." Chance hopped into the back of the SUV and reached his hand out to Luke, who crawled in after him. "I'm not going to complain about getting to spend time with you without lots of people around us."

Sitting in the rear of Chance's Tahoe, it felt like they were the only two people in the world right now. "Me too."

Soon Luke wandered over to get their popcorn and drinks as Chance paired his phone to the movie theater's unique radio frequency, and by the time he got back, the trailers were nearly over. "Did I miss anything good?" he asked, hopping back inside.

"They made another James Bond movie," Chance said. "We can come back here and see it if you want."

He's planning our next date. Luke grinned and ate some popcorn. "That sounds good."

By mid-movie, Luke had figured out that it was the butler who had killed off the family patriarch and nearly made off with the fortune, but he couldn't have explained any more of the plot than that. All his attention was focused on Chance, and how it felt, their bodies touching as they sat in the back of the Tahoe and watched the movie. Right now, Chance's arm stretched out behind him, nearly all the way across Luke's back, and he tucked himself comfortably against that arm.

Just then, the screen erupted in light as an eighteen-wheeler truck exploded. Luke inhaled quickly at the shock and turned his face away from the jarring sounds and toward Chance. This close, he saw a light smattering of freckles dusted across Chance's cheeks, and suddenly, he wanted to kiss Chance very badly.

Had he said that aloud? Luke wasn't sure, but just as that thought crossed his mind, Chance bent down toward him and brushed their lips together. Luke's hand reached for the back of Chance's head, and he tilted his head the other direction, deepening the kiss.

A minute later they separated, both slightly out of breath and smiling. "I was correct," Luke said, his thumb stroking Chance's jaw.

Those bright blue eyes widened. "About what?" he asked, pressing another soft kiss to Luke's cheek.

"The fireworks." Luke turned his head and caught Chance's mouth for another kiss. "I remembered fireworks that first time."

"Oh," Chance grinned, his thumb rubbing along Luke's bottom lip. "Still there?"

Luke nodded. "Definitely." He curled his body toward Chance and pulled him close, nuzzling his throat and dropping kisses along his jaw.

After the movie ended, they shifted to the front seat, and kissed a little longer as they waited for the parking lot to empty. Sweet, endless kisses that Luke was already addicted to after one date. But soon the traffic died down, and it was time to head home.

Chance's hand reached out and held Luke's as they drove, which both terrified and thrilled Luke. When they pulled up in front of Luke's house, Chance turned toward him. "Thank you for coming out with me tonight."

"Thank you for inviting me." Luke never brought people back to his house and felt unsure what the correct next step would be. But Chance leaned forward for one more goodnight kiss before he pulled back with a quiet groan. "Can I call you tomorrow?"

"Yes, please." They both smiled, and Luke opened the door and stepped outside.

Chance waited at the curb until Luke made it inside, then drove away.

"How was the movie?" Jessica asked as Luke set his keys down on the front table. She sat cross-legged on the sofa watching a TV show, but her face broke out into a grin at the expression on his face. "Never mind. I'm guessing you had something else on your mind."

Someone on his mind, Luke thought to himself. And on his lips.

Chapter Fourteen

Sunshine filled Chance's bedroom when his eyes finally blinked open. Sheba sat on the pillow next to him, examining him with his large, green eyes. His hand reached out, and Sheba butted his head playfully against it. "Sorry, sweetheart. Late breakfast today." His throaty purr told him he didn't mind, and after Chance took a quick trip to the bathroom, Sheba followed him to the kitchen area for his morning meal.

Chance made himself a cup of coffee and headed back to his bed and retrieved his phone. He checked his calendar. *No rest for the wicked.* Even on Sunday, he had responsibilities that took up most of his day. First, Sunday brunch with his parents that he couldn't get out of, no matter how much he didn't want to go. Then an organizational meeting with Valley View Pride Center about their upcoming festival. But Chance needed to carve out some time for Luke in there if he could. Even if they couldn't see each other, he wanted to talk to the other man, to see how he was doing and gauge if Luke was as excited about the possibility of something special between them as he was.

When was the last time he'd had a night like that? Dinner and a movie, yes, but so much more. Those sweet kisses, holding hands, and then holding each other. Nothing about Luke made Chance feel like he was out to get anything from him, or that his motives were anything but genuine. Luke liked him, really liked him. *Why is that so hard to believe?* Maybe Chance had just been off the market so long that he forgot what it was like, being kissed and touched. Being wanted.

All he knew was that now he wanted more—anything and everything that Luke wanted to offer.

There were two text messages when he stepped out of the shower, but neither of them from Luke.

> Nolan: *How did the date go? [gif of Bugs Bunny making a kissing face]*

> Mom: *Country club at 11:00. See you soon.*

He rolled his eyes. The idea of country clubs still existing boggled him, but his father liked the golf course, and his mother enjoyed the preferential exclusivity.

· · · · · **·** · · · ·

At a quarter after eleven, Chance parked his Tahoe and jogged toward the club's restaurant, where his parents were already seated. "Sorry I'm late," he announced, and kissed his mother on the cheek. "There was an accident on the interstate. How was your game?" he asked his dad.

"Three under par," Donavan 'Don' Edwards III chuckled. "But it was better than Tim McTavish at least. They've got a new groundskeeper, and he isn't quite up to scruff like old Reggie was." He blew on his coffee before taking a sip. "You should join us sometime. You used to like to golf."

"Yeah, I might." Chance knew he should. Those had been fun mornings with his father, back when he was younger. Chance remembered driving the carts around and feeling like a grown-up, then sharing a burger and fries in the golf center's snack bar. "Let's try to find some time soon."

His mother beamed listening to them talk. Marcia Edwards reached out and rested her manicured hand on Chance's arm. "Your father and I are driving down to Galveston on Saturday morning. Your Aunt Amanda, well—" Marcia shared a knowing glance with her husband, who just chuckled. "You know your aunt, dear. She's planned a big luncheon at noon and then the dinner party starts at seven in the evening. Do you want to drive with us?"

Chance shook his head. "I'll head down myself. I've promised to help with Rainbow's rescue organization on Saturday morning, but I should be done by one or two, and that's plenty of time to make it to Nanna's party that night."

Immediately his mother's mood changed, and the temperature at the table dropped with her frigid tones. "I asked you to be available to your family this weekend. Your grandmother's eightieth birthday party has been scheduled for months and several of us have worked hard to create a joyful experience for her. You know she loves having all her family around her, and you have always been her favorite grandchild."

Just once, could they ever have a conversation that didn't end up with his mother trying to make Chance feel guilty about something? "And I'll be at the party," Chance repeated, and settled back into his chair. "I wouldn't miss Nanna's birthday for the world."

"Amanda will be disappointed. I told her you'd be there all day," she snapped. His father coughed into his napkin and reached for his coffee again.

Chance shook his head. "I wish you hadn't." Aunt Amanda was married to his father's youngest brother and had tried to introduce Chance to several potential marriage partners over the years, as his family dismissed his sexual preference as a phase.

Right on cue— "Any new young ladies in your life?" Marcia asked.

Time to change the subject. Chance turned toward his father. "How is your work going? Anything new in human cardiology these days?" Yes, it was rude to ignore his mother's question, but she hadn't really expected an answer, had she?

Don set his fork down and wiped his mouth but smiled at his son. "Busy, never stops. But Dr. Warrick just retired a few months ago, and now your mother and I have talked about when it will be my turn."

Retirement. "That's crazy. I guess I thought you'd be at that practice forever."

Don chuckled. "As did I, but we'll see. They've hired a replacement for Sam, and she's young, probably close to your age. It makes me think about hanging it up soon too. There's something appealing about having more free time to spend with my mother, making sure she's taken care of down there." He reached his hand and covered his wife's hand, as she beamed at him. "And your mother and I might do some travel."

"Oh, it's been ages since we've been to Europe, but there's always so much to do with the Edwards Foundation." Marcia spent much of her time working on various foundation committees, hosting galas and banquets. "Perhaps if our son finally took a position within the foundation, that might free up a little more time for you and me, sweetheart."

Unbelievable. "We'll see," was as much as Chance gave his mother. As if adding another duty to his plate would improve his life.

Right now, the only thing he wanted to spend more time on was getting to know Luke better.

Chapter Fifteen

"I thought about your suggestion for the travel application, about automatically adding the geolocator to the images, and talked to Meredith about it. She's on board, so go ahead and make whatever changes you think are best."

Luke glanced over at the second monitor on his workstation momentarily. "I'm glad to hear that, Russell," he said, his fingers continuing to type as his eyes returned to the main screen with his current coding project.

The face on the other end laughed. "You've already changed the code, haven't you?" When Luke's lips curled up at the corners, the other man chuckled louder. "I trust you, Luke. Just have it ready for us by the deadline, and all will be golden." Russell's brows furrowed. "Dude—did you get a haircut?"

Luke stopped typing. "I did," he said with a momentary pause before he resumed typing.

Russell whistled low. "I've known you for seven years, Luke. A haircut means a job interview or a date, and I know you're successful enough with your freelance programming business and don't want to be tied to corporate bullshit anymore." His smile widened. "Spill the beans. What's his name?"

Luke considered turning off the monitor, but Russell was correct—they'd been friends for a long time. "His name is Chance, and we've gone out on one date. Tonight, I am going to his house, and he's making dinner for us." Luke's lips quirked. "I am meeting his cat."

Russell laughed again. "That's a big step! And handy in the kitchen, that's always a positive sign. Handsome?" Luke didn't answer again but couldn't help the smile. "My goodness, Luke, I want you to be happy, you know that, but make sure you get the project done on time before you ride off into the sunset with your Prince Charming."

"Have I ever been late on a deadline?" Luke asked, turning his attention back to the second monitor and Russell.

"Not once." Russell's face perked up. "That reminds me, I've got the inside scoop on the opening night screening of the new Planet Zombie movie, the one from the video game."

"I'm familiar with Planet Zombie," Luke said. It was one of his all-time favorite video games. "I still can't believe they turned it into a movie."

Russell snorted. "Every IP is up for grabs these days. Anyway, the director lives here in Austin, and he's doing a big premiere when it comes out. I can get you tickets if you want. It'll be a huge event, and most of the film's stars are going to be here."

Oh. "I'll wait and see it in a few weeks, once the crowds die down." Luke couldn't believe the opportunity he was missing, but just the idea of being with all those screaming, yelling fans, hundreds of people he didn't know in a darkened room made his skin crawl. There was no way he could do it. "But thank you. I appreciate the offer."

Russell snapped his fingers and pointed at Luke. "Oh yeah, I forgot. Anyway, the offer stands in case, you know…" They said their goodbyes, and Luke spent another hour working before he closed his software programs, all his work done for the day. He wanted time to play with the dogs and then shower before their date that evening.

· · · · ● · ● · · · ·

Chance had told him to pull around the back of the office building where the clinic was located and park next to his Tahoe. Luke understood once he arrived. Cars were still in the parking lot, belonging to Dr. Berry, Norma, and Gigi, he assumed. Luke hoped Chance was most likely not embarrassed by their burgeoning relationship but understood discretion and the desire to keep some things private, at least for now.

Luke: *I'm here.*

A moment later, Chance walked out from a door on the far side of the building. "Hey there," Chance called out, and led Luke into the building and up a narrow stairwell. "I keep that door locked all the time, so no one can get into my place," Chance said at the top of the stairs. He opened a tall door, and Luke followed him inside.

Luke's eyes went wide when he saw Chance's studio apartment. "This is incredible." It wasn't a lot of square footage, but all opened up into one extremely large studio that took up the most of the second floor of the building. A giant flat-screen television mounted on a wall in front of a comfortable-looking sofa took up one side of the room, across from a full kitchen with a dining table. Off in the furthest corner of the apartment, Luke spotted a large bed.

Chance was clearly pleased to show this off to Luke. "Remind me to take you up to the rooftop."

"Oh, most certainly." Luke was in awe as he walked around. Having spent nearly the last twenty-four hours in his bedroom/office, Luke felt immature compared to someone who had his life under control.

Just then, a black cat leapt down off a bookshelf onto the dining table, gazing up cautiously at Luke. "Hello there," Luke said as he greeted Chance's pet. He held out his hand and smiled as the cat rubbed its face against him.

Chance grinned. "This is Sheba."

"Sheba." Luke's lips quirked. "That's quite a name. Beautiful."

"Handsome," Chance said, and offered Luke a bottle of beer. "Sheba is a boy, so he's handsome."

"That means I'll be having dinner with two handsome men tonight." Luke watched as Sheba jumped off the table and strolled toward the sofa. He glanced back at the kitchen. "Something smells amazing."

Chance flushed pink, those bright eyes shining. "Thank you. Everything is simmering right now." He stepped back, walking toward another staircase. "We've got some time now, I guess. Let me show you upstairs."

The rooftop patio was Chance's pride and joy, that was obvious from his expression. He'd cleaned it up, put some wooden benches in, and some plants and small container trees. This time of night, the street below them was full of people walking to neighborhood restaurants and bars, and out in the distance, downtown Houston lit up like a jewel.

Luke took another drink from his beer bottle and glanced around. "This is incredible," he said, his voice low. "I would have never guessed all this was up here." Glancing over the edge, he turned back to Chance. "I didn't expect this from you."

Chance looked down too, the hustle and bustle of the street below them, with people walking in and out of the local restaurants and coffee shops. "I don't know how I ended up here, other than just landing in the right place at the right time." Chance snorted. "And I guess it doesn't hurt when your family owns the building."

"I was about to ask how this happened." Chance was so down to earth that it was easy to forget that he came from great wealth.

Dinner was pot roast with mashed potatoes and grilled carrots, and they ate their fill as they talked about their day. Luke described the changes he wanted to make to the travel app he was currently working on, and Chance described a close call with a Chihuahua who escaped her yard and got hit by a car. "I was so grateful that Clara happened to show up early for work today. I spent a lot of time on those lacerations, and she handled the rest of the clients all on her own until the dog was splinted up and ready to head home." A long day, but it ended up well in the end. "I didn't want to tell those kids that their pet was gone."

"My hero," Luke said. "You saved them too. The emotional impact of a pet's death, especially a preventable one, would be significant to any child."

Chance blushed and tried to wave off Luke's compliments. "All in a day's work."

"And then you found time to cook this meal. It's fantastic, and quite the step up from my ramen noodle lunch."

Chance looked mildly horrified, then stood and began clearing the plates. "I've got a surprise for you for dessert." Together they cleaned the kitchen. Luke filled the dishwasher as Chance put all the leftovers away, including a small plastic container for Luke to take home. "So you won't have ramen noodles again tomorrow," Chance said with a smirk.

Once they finished, Chance reached into a drawer and pulled out two spoons. Then he plucked a pint of Blue Bell Peach Cobbler ice cream out of the freezer. "Got room?"

Luke's jaw dropped. "You remembered."

They walked toward the living room, and after settling on a very comfortable sofa, Chance turned on some music and offered Luke the pint. "You weren't kidding about it being a popular flavor. It took me a couple stores before I found it."

Luke's spoon dug into the ice cream, and he lifted it to his mouth—cold and peachy and perfect. "It's so good." He scooped up another spoonful and held this one up for Chance. Luke watched intently as Chance opened his mouth, his pink tongue darting out to catch the ice cream, then the spoon disappeared between his lips.

Luke did it again, mesmerized by the sight.

After they finished the pint, Chance tilted his head and stole a kiss, and Luke tasted the peachy flavor on Chance's lips.

One kiss led to another, and soon they lay tangled on the sofa, breathless. But Luke caught Chance stifling a yawn. He glanced at his phone. It was almost ten PM. No doubt Chance's day had been a long one, too. Maybe that yawn meant it was time for Luke to leave?

Luke surprised himself with how much he wanted to stay with Chance and see where the evening led, but that was selfish. He handed the empty container back to Chance with a wistful sigh. "I'd suppose I'd better be going. Thank you for showing me all of this. You have a beautiful home hidden away here."

Chance nodded, but something shadowed his eyes—was that disappointment? But it was too soon, right? Too soon to expect anything more than dinner. The fact that Luke was even thinking about it being too soon meant it was too soon.

"Luke?" He looked up. Chance was staring at him, and Luke realized he'd drifted a thousand miles away. Chance leaned in closer and nosed against Luke's jaw. "Don't go."

Luke closed his eyes at that touch, Chance's scent in his nostrils. "You sure?" he asked.

Chance bent his head and kissed Luke, soft and slow, his hand snaking around Luke's waist. Luke's hands wound across Chance's back. Chance tugged on Luke's hands, as they made their way across the room and into Chance's bed, most of their clothing dropping off along the way. Luke's feet didn't touch the ground until the back of his legs hit the bed, and when Chance pushed him back lightly, he tumbled down backward onto the big bed, his arms stretched wide as Chance crawled above him, kissing his neck, his jaw, his chest.

It was heaven. Luke tilted his chin up, offering more skin up to Chance's wandering mouth. His own hands slid along Chance's strong arms, lightly muscled. Was that a tattoo on his back?

Luke would have to investigate that more later.

Chance lowered his body, pressing their groins together, and they rocked against each other for a few strokes. Then Luke reached around Chance. "Hold on," he whispered, and rolled them both over so that he was on top, Chance's gorgeous body below him.

The wide grin on Chance's face, and the hard, leaking cock pressing into his thigh told Luke that they both were enjoying this. Luke's hands slid downward, though he stopped to tweak a hard pink nipple, then ran his fingers through the soft trail of hair leading down from Chance's navel to his flushed cock.

"Oh—" Chance's bright blue eyes fluttered closed when Luke's fingers wrapped around his cock and began stroking it. "Luke, God," Chance groaned, his back arching under Luke's hand.

All the blood rushed to Luke's head, and he closed his eyes, dizzy. Was he really here? Was he the man holding Chance, kissing Chance, the one who made Chance feel like this? Those thoughts were soon dashed away, replaced by blinding pleasure as Chance's hand gripped Luke's cock, and their mouths found each other again.

Luke knew he was going to come first, and it wasn't long before he bit down on Chance's shoulder, shuddering his release in long, sticky pulses over Chance's fingers. His own hand paused briefly before he continued stroking Chance's long shaft, as he learned that rhythm that Chance liked. Chance's face contorted, almost a grimace, and when he came Luke brushed their lips together, so he felt Chance's soft whine against his mouth, his hand now wet and warm.

For a few minutes, neither man spoke, and Luke lay still, staring at the pipework in the industrial ceiling above them. "Hey." Chance reached out and touched his cheek. "Are you okay?"

"Yeah." Luke stretched as Chance sat up and tossed his legs over the bed. He reached down and picked up his discarded cotton boxers and cleaned his hand, then offered them to Luke.

Luke cleared his throat as he tidied up and wished it wasn't this awkward. "So, I guess—"

Chance took the boxers and tossed them back on the floor, then reached for Luke's hand. "Do you need to go home?" he asked and pushed a stray hair off of Luke's forehead.

That hopeful expression on Chance's face made Luke's heart twist. He rested one hand on Chance's thigh and took a deep breath. A hand job was one thing; spending the night was another, at least as far as Luke was concerned. "I don't need to." Another penetrating look at Chance and that unspoken question in his eyes. "Are you certain? If my car is still parked beside yours in the morning, people will ask questions."

Chance nodded and laid down next to Luke. Those long arms wound around Luke, their legs tangled, and Luke sighed contentedly to himself. When was the last time he allowed himself to do this? When had either of them had this, a moment of lazy lovemaking with someone they trusted?

Chance turned out to be a snuggler, which shouldn't have surprised Luke, and he rested his head against Luke's shoulder, nosing his chest while Luke traced the well-defined muscle of Chance's arm with his fingers. "You were wrong, you know," Luke murmured.

"How?" Chance asked and kissed his temple.

He lifted his face toward Chance. "You are most definitely a man, and you are beautiful." They kissed again as Luke tucked against Chance's side. *A perfect fit.* Luke closed his eyes, Chance's scent new but comforting.

Sheba settled on the edge of the bed, and Luke smiled. His arms tightened around Chance, and they fell asleep.

Chapter Sixteen

Sure enough, it didn't take long for the questions to get started. "I thought I saw Luke Granger's car in the back lot last night when we left. Were there any problems with Sadie's leg?" Norma asked coyly as she set her bag down when they arrived for work. Gigi poked her head through the door to hear the answer.

Chance took a quick sip from his coffee mug and burned his tongue in the process. "Ouch," he murmured, and looked around for a napkin. "Give me a moment." Norma handed him a paper towel, her expression frank and hopeful. "Yes, Luke was at my apartment last night. I made him dinner."

Both women squealed. "What did you make?" Gigi asked and leaned against the wall, fully invested in this conversation.

"Not the question I expected, to be honest," Chance said, wiping the coffee from his scrub top. "But pot roast and veggies."

That seemed to be the right answer because both of them smiled and nodded in approval. "When are you going to see each other next?" Gigi asked.

Chance shrugged. "We haven't talked about a specific date. Maybe this Saturday."

Norma frowned and folded her arms in front of her. "But you've got that thing in Galveston this weekend."

Damn, Chance had forgotten all about his grandmother's birthday party on Saturday night. "You're right. Maybe sometime next week then." The idea of not seeing Luke for several days, not kissing him or holding him in his arms was like a punch in the gut. *I'm in deep*, he thought, but it felt good, after so long without those desires.

Norma turned back to prepping the exam rooms, but Gigi had other ideas. "Is it too soon to ask Mr. Granger to go with you?" she asked.

"Probably," Chance said, and took another sip from his coffee mug. "If it was just me, maybe. But this is a family event, and I'm sure nothing will send him running faster than being around my family."

Gigi rolled her eyes. "They can't all be bad, Doctor Chance. Or maybe you two could go down a day early and just spend some time with each other. Nothing's more romantic than a weekend trip together." She closed her eyes and sighed. "Those big hotel beds, and eating out at fancy restaurants, and just playing tourist together. It's the Fourth of July weekend too, so there'll probably be lots of fireworks you can watch, sitting on the beach and snuggling with each other."

Chance considered her words. True, there were some good cousins out there, and he loved his grandmother dearly. "I'll think about it," he said, and grinned as she scurried to the front when the door chimes went off. Norma headed back to the large exam room, but from her facial expression it was clear she'd listened to their conversation. "What do you think?"

Norma took a deep breath and shrugged. "A weekend at the coast sounds like fun, but your time will be split between your new boyfriend and your family. Someone is going to feel let down, that's what I'd worry about," she said, then headed toward the front to check-in the first patient of the day.

The busy morning flew by, and before Chance knew it, it was lunch time. He pulled out his pot roast leftovers, and after heating it up in the microwave, he snapped a photo and sent it to Luke with a text message. *Thinking about you.*

Luke responded immediately with a photo of his own, displaying an empty plastic container. *It was delicious.* He sent another photograph, this one of Sadie, sleeping on a pillow on his bed, her head still encased in an e-collar.

Ignore the unmade bed and general messy state of my 'office' please.

Chance was about to respond when another text message came through and caught his attention.

> Charlotte: *Hey there C*
>
> Charlotte*: your mother said you weren't bringing anyone to Nanna's party. Can I catch a ride down to Galveston with you on Saturday? <kissy face emoji>*

Chance stared at his phone for a long time before he moved. Were they still trying this? Did his parents and Charlotte's parents think, after all these years, that something romantic would magically spring up between them? Charlotte Foxworthy was tall, blonde, and rich. She should have no trouble finding a husband, and yet she, along with her family, seemed to set their cap on Chance, as if one day he'd decide that he wasn't gay anymore.

As if.

> Chance: *Sorry, you heard wrong. I'm bringing my boyfriend to the party. I'll see you there.*

Boyfriend? *Why had he texted that?*

Chance looked down at his phone and noted the time—twelve minutes past eleven. "I'll give her ten minutes," he said to himself.

Eight minutes later, Chance's phone rang. "Hello Mom," he said, and headed to the sink to wash his dish.

"When were you going to mention that you were bringing someone to Nanna's party?" Marcia asked, ignoring his greeting.

Chance sighed, already regretting his impulsive text to Charlotte. "I didn't know I had to tell the party committee that I needed a Plus One to my grandmother's birthday party."

"Don't take that tone with me, Chance. You know this is an important event for all the family."

"And the Foxworthys too, it seems," Chance murmured.

"They are close friends of your grandmother and have always supported the foundation."

Chance's brow arched at that comment, but he pushed that aside right now. "Well, let this be my official notification. I am bringing someone. Also, I'm not marrying Charlotte Foxworthy."

"One of these days, you are going to have to take your place within the family, Chance, or you are going to find yourself pushed out of it. I'm trying my hardest to keep you in your Nanna's good graces, but if you want to be disowned, so be it."

The phone went silent, and Chance set it down as if it was poison. Disowned? Never once in his life had his grandmother or any other member of the family talked about him being disowned because he was gay.

Maybe his mother knew something that he didn't. *Maybe I shouldn't go this weekend*, he thought. Or is that just want they wanted him to do—to put distance between the Edwards family matriarch and her favorite grandchild.

Chance rubbed his head. All this ridiculous nonsense and all Chance wanted to do was wish his grandmother a happy birthday. But now he'd looped Luke in on this turmoil as well.

Norma appeared in front of him, holding a clipboard and laughing. "We've got ferrets in room one. They're super cute but wiggly." She peered closely at him. "What's wrong?"

"Nothing." Chance took a deep breath and pasted a smile on his face. "You know, my mother. The usual." He took the clipboard from her and walked into her room and wondered how he was going to convince the guy he was dating—who hated crowds of strangers—to come meet the parents.

And fifty other family members.

Chapter Seventeen

Luke didn't own a suitcase, so he borrowed one from Jessica—purple with glittery stars and sparkles. Still, it wasn't like anyone was going to see it but Chance, and Luke couldn't imagine Chance caring much about what his luggage looked like.

Not when there were other things to think about, like spending time together in that big hotel bed.

That reminded him—*underwear*. He opened his top dresser drawer, scavenging through his many pairs of old, stretched out boxer briefs to see what he had that was presentable. Finally, he spotted some bright red low rise briefs, the kind with the pouch for the cock. They'd been a gag gift from Jess one year, and now he threw them into the suitcase that lay open on his bed.

"Packing?" Jessica stood in his doorway, then barged in and sat on the bed. She eyed the underwear and smiled. "This is a big weekend for you two, eh?"

He ignored the question and closed the suitcase lid. "I need your help."

That got her attention. Jessica straightened up, curious. "Of course. What do you need?"

Luke looked at his closet again, spreading his hands wide. "What do I wear to a fancy family dinner?"

"It's not formal, is it? Black tie? Sit down dinner?" Jess asked, but Luke shook his head. She slid off the bed and stood next to Luke, peering into the closet. "Tell me you have shoes that aren't sneakers."

Luke sighed. "I was going to purchase new ones, depending on what I wore. But these—" He bend down and selected a pair of fairly clean Keds. "They're considered dressy sneakers. I don't suppose that counts."

Jessica's eye twitched. "You need a new pair of loafers or dress shoes. Nice boots would also be acceptable." She slid several shirts around until she found the one that she wanted—a blue long-sleeved shirt she picked out for him on their first-date shopping trip. Stepping deeper into the closet, she reached for a dark gray suit pushed to the far end and pulled it out, dusting off the shoulders. "Does this still fit you?" Her face fell, and her voice dropped. "I bet you haven't touched it since the funeral."

She was right. "It fits." Luke paused, his eyes narrowing as he stared at the suit. "It *should* fit."

"Do me a favor and double check before you pack it, but my advice is to take the whole suit. You might be able to get away with this shirt and the jacket, and a nice pair of khakis, but have the pants there just in case. I'd take them both and see what Chance is wearing."

Luke set the shirt and suit next to each other, then pulled out his phone and took a picture. He'd go shop for shoes tomorrow. "Thank you. I appreciate the help."

"No problem." Jessica sat back down on the bed. "Are you nervous about this trip?" Luke bit his lip but didn't answer. She shook her head. "I'm talking about the party, you dork. Meeting his family. You haven't met any of them yet, have you?"

"No." Chance's parents lived in Houston, but this would be the first time Luke was introduced to them, along with his grandmother, aunts and uncles, and assorted cousins. "I get tossed to the lions all at once."

"What do you know about them?"

Luke sat down on the bed next to her. "His grandmother's turning eighty, so everyone who can make it is going to be in attendance. She's the matriarch and quite wealthy. Chance thinks it will be quite a sight, watching everyone vie for her attention."

Now it was Jessica's turn to frown, and her eyes darkened with worry. "You don't sound like you're looking forward to it."

She was right. "I'm looking forward to spending time with Chance and getting to know him better. He made reservations at a very nice hotel in town overlooking the beach. But—" Luke's eyes found Jessica's, anxiety all over his face. "There's a lot of new people to meet. I don't want to mess this up and disappoint him."

Jessica reached for his hand and squeezed it tight in hers. "Yeah. It would make more sense if you guys had dated longer. You know, you could always tell him that you can't go. Make up some excuse or blame me. Say that I need you here this weekend." She reached out and put her arm around him. "Or you could be honest with him, and say that you don't want to, not yet. You think he'd be pissed?"

"I don't know." Luke laughed, a bitter note in his tone. "I guess that's the point. We don't know each other all that well yet. Just two guys that have had a crush on each other for a long time. Two dates." It didn't sound like that much, but already Luke was ready to do this if it was what Chance wanted of him.

"Luke—" Jessica rested her head on his shoulder. "Do you think this is a good idea? Maybe you shouldn't go, not this year." She squeezed his hand. "If things go well, you can go to Grandma's party next year."

Luke heard her words, but just the idea of telling Chance that he didn't want to go had his stomach tied up in knots. All he'd ever wanted was to see those blue eyes looking at him with love and affection. How could he turn down such a personal request? "I'll be okay."

She didn't look like she believed him but didn't say any more about the subject. "Okay, then we've got the party outfit almost done. What about a swimsuit? Do you have something nice for the hotel pool? Or are you two hitting the beach?"

Luke blushed. "The one I currently own is kind of—ratty, so I ordered a new one online. It should arrive tomorrow."

Jessica's face wrinkled in confusion, but she shook her head and chuckled. "Only you would pick out a bathing suit over the internet."

"It had many positive reviews." Luke frowned when she busted out into laughter. "I don't understand what's funny about that."

"You're just so—" Jessica reached over and kissed his cheek. "Never stop being you, Luke." She stood and started out of his room.

"Jess." She paused and turned. "What do you have planned this weekend?" he asked, curious after she mentioned that he could use her as an excuse.

Jess shrugged. "You know the Fourth of July holiday. Lots of dogs somehow manage to escape their yards when all those fireworks go off." Her lips curled into a smile. "You hate to see it happen to some of these shitty dog owners."

Luke sighed. "What do you have planned? Please tell me you aren't going to do something foolish. Or worse," he added. "Illegal."

"Don't ask, and I won't tell." Jessica smiled warmly at him again. "You don't worry about me. We've got a plan. You just go enjoy the beach and your cute vet boyfriend. I'm sure his family will love you."

"I'd be happy if they tolerated me," Luke said, but turned back toward his closet as Jessica headed down the hall. The more he looked at the suit and shirt combo, the more he liked it.

Now all he needed was new shoes—and maybe a few of those anti-anxiety pills that he kept in his bathroom drawer for emergencies.

Chapter Eighteen

The ladies at End of the Rainbow Rescues understood when Chance told them that he was unable to help out with their adoption drive on Saturday morning, especially when someone (one of the twins, probably) spilled the beans that was he was taking his new boyfriend to the coast for the weekend. Clara waved her hand at him when he offered to take the morning shift on Friday so they could drive down when he got off at three. "Take the whole day, Chance. You covered this place for me when I was gone for a week. It's the least I could do for you and Luke."

His stomach did somersaults when people talked about him and Luke, but it felt good, knowing his friends wanted him to be happy.

Chance had lived a little over an hour from the Texas coast all his life, but the only time he ever made the trip to Galveston was to see his grandmother. They had always been close, and he eagerly looked forward to spending time with her at her birthday party. But his stomach rumbled with nervous energy as he and Luke drove south down Interstate 45. "Did I mention I'm glad you came with me?" he asked for the third time since he'd picked Luke up late Friday morning.

Luke's brow arched, but he just nodded. "You did. And I'm glad you invited me." His eyes fell back down to his lap, thumbs darting wildly as he played on his Nintendo Switch. "Tell me again who will be there."

Chance took a breath. "All of my grandmother's children, and there's five of them—so my dad, his sisters Alice and Jayne, and his brothers David and Bruce. Any of them that are married will bring their spouses. All of them have at least one kid, so there are the cousins. Some of them have kids now too." He took another deep breath and chuckled. "That's the official family. But there will be a few others that'll most likely be there, friends of the family that we grew up with. Unofficial cousins, stuff like that. All in all, I'm guessing about fifty people at the party."

Luke went silent a moment. Then— "Fifty people, wow. I don't think I even know fifty people."

Chance reached out and touched Luke's shoulder briefly before returning to the steering wheel. "I told you, we can leave any time you want. I just want to wish my grandma a happy birthday and let her know that I showed up for her party. We wouldn't be able to have any special time together anyway, with all those other around us, so she'll understand if I don't stay long. I think she'd like meeting you, too, so if you want, we'll stop by the next morning if she's up to visitors."

A small smile creeped onto Luke's face. "Okay. Um, is there anything I should know? Skeletons in any closet I need to avoid opening?" he asked.

Chance snorted. "You're dating the biggest skeleton—the gay grandson."

Luke's eyes went wide, his game forgotten for the moment. "Please tell me this is not how you're telling the whole family that you're gay?"

"Oh no, they all know. It's a sore subject for some of them, but one that I've never shied away from." He'd allowed them to ignore his sexuality in the past, but no more. Chance didn't want to be that man.

Luke relaxed in his seat, but he'd stopped playing his game. Instead, his eyes lingered on the landscape as they drove, the ground growing marshier, patches of water sprouting around everywhere. "Do your parents know I'm coming?"

"They know I'm bringing someone." This was probably a conversation they should have had before they left, probably even when Chance invited Luke to come with him. "We don't have to stay long at the party. In fact, I'm sure it will be boring, and we can head out whenever you're ready.

I just want to see my grandmother. The rest are just—"
Chance waved his hand back and forth. "The rest of the
weekend is just you and me."

They checked into the beautiful high-rise hotel right off
the beach just after midday and headed up to their junior
suite on the ninth floor. "Whoa," Luke murmured as he
followed Chance inside.

The spacious living area had a large sofa facing a
wall-mounted television, with additional seats and a writ-
ing desk in the corner. Chance walked into the bedroom
and dropped their luggage on the large white bed, then
walked over to the window and spread open the heavy gold
curtains, exposing a private balcony with patio chairs. It
was a perfect day, a few puffy white clouds over the Gulf
of Mexico, and he spotted crowds of people playing in the
water. "Not too bad."

"Not bad at all. Come check this out," Luke called from
the living room. He held up a basket that had been left on
a table in their room. Fruits, bags of nuts, and a couple
bottles of beer, along with a typed letter fastened to the
top. "This sounds like my Aunt Amanda," he said, and
passed the note to Luke.

*Welcome to the birthday celebration weekend honoring
Evelyn Brightwell Edwards! Below is the itinerary for Saturday and Sunday. Please let me know if there are any*

events you will not be attending, as a reservation has already been made in your name. Ciao!

Below was a list of events—Saturday lunch at noon at Beachcombers Bistro, a restaurant at the local country club, with golf tee times scheduled afterward for the men and spa treatments for the women, culminating with the official start of Evelyn Edwards eightieth birthday party at seven. Sunday brunch at Marcelino's Grille capped off events the next morning before people headed home. Chance shook his head and laughed. *How had she figured out where they were staying?* "Aunt Mandy is—organized. Think World War II general levels of organization."

Luke's eyes twinkled in amusement, and his shoulders relaxed. "I can see that. Do we need to do *all* of that?" he asked, hesitation in his voice.

"Nope, not unless you want." Chance's hand found Luke's, and he laced their fingers together. He kissed the side of Luke's head, warmed that Luke was willing to participate in those events if Chance wanted to. "We came here for the party, and to spend time together." Chance reached into his pocket and handed Luke the extra door key card. "None of that starts until tomorrow, anyway. I wanted you all to myself today." He snaked an arm around Luke's waist again, pulling him tight. "Anything you want to do first? We can go get some lunch and go sit by the pool or go drive around if there's something you'd rather do while we're here on the island."

They ended up crossing the busy street and walked along the Seawall until they found a seaside restaurant that looked good and wasn't too crowded. The fish and chips were hot and delicious as they sat on a balcony overlooking the gulf water.

"Want to go play on the beach for a little bit?" Chance asked after the server came and cleared their plates. Luke peered out at the crowded beaches, and his brows furrowed. Holiday weekend, Chance realized, and added, "Or we can just hang out at the pool tomorrow. Might be fewer people there."

Luke nodded and grinned. "I'd like that."

After lunch, Luke spotted a kiosk where they could rent electric bikes. Chance laughed but soon they were cycling up the long Seawall, stopping every few minutes when Luke saw some shells to pick up, or a mural that he wanted to photograph. Chance pointed at an amusement park a few blocks away as they headed back to their bikes. "We can go check that out if it doesn't look too crowded. Last one there buys the cotton candy."

"You're still hungry?" Luke snorted, but he managed to get on his bike first and had a significant lead as they rode toward the pier.

The sun was setting as they made it back to their hotel that evening, arms filled with shopping bags and leftovers from their excellent seafood dinner. They rode the elevator alone back up to the seventh floor, both quiet, but it was a comfortable silence.

Chance opened the door to their room, and the frigidly cold air hit him after spending the day in the warmth of the July sun. "You got some color on your cheeks," he said to Luke as he walked past.

Luke glanced at himself in the mirror and made an appraising face. "A little bit." But he had that same nervous energy that they'd both had all evening, as if they knew what was going to happen when they got back to the hotel.

"Looks good on you." Chance stepped behind Luke and rested his head on Luke's shoulder. "You okay?" he asked, butterflies fluttering in his own stomach. "There's a rooftop bar on the top floor of this place. We can go get a drink if you want."

Luke shook his head. "I'm okay. Just—" He smiled and kicked off his shoes. "It's been a long day."

Chance froze. Did Luke not want to— "Oh, yeah. I guess you might be kinda tired by all that stuff we did."

But Luke's eyes warmed as they met Chance's, and it was like that night after their first date, that hum of electricity and desire between them. "I'm not tired," Luke said, and reached for Chance's hand. Now his eyes blazed with heat. "But I am ready to go to bed."

They were both nervous about this, but Chance swallowed, admiring Luke's bravery in this. Just like that night in his apartment, it was Luke who took the lead here, as he tugged Chance toward the bed. Chance pulled Luke's t-shirt off over his head as Luke unbuttoned Chance's shirt. "Tell me what you want," Chance whispered. At this moment, he'd do anything, everything that Luke wanted. "What do you need?"

"I want you inside me." Luke's words, low and soft, and they cut through the quiet hotel room. Chance groaned in response. "I want to feel you tomorrow, while we're around everyone else." Their lips met in a soft, wet kiss. "I want to know who I belong to."

Fuck. Chance's cock went hard as a rock. "Yes," he said, unable to keep the smile off his face as they kissed again. "Anything. Everything." His shaking hands unzipped Luke's shorts. One hand snaked inside and pressed against that hard cock, the wet spot already starting on Luke's underwear. "You wanna come before or after we fuck?" Chance asked, kissing Luke's neck as his hand curled around Luke's shaft. "Or while I'm inside you?"

Now it was Luke's turn to growl. He kissed Chance harder, and his own hands tugged the shirt off Chance's shoulders. Soon those hands settled on Chance's hips and pulled him close. "Yes, that last one." One more soft kiss before Luke slid on top of the bed, holding his hand out to Chance. "I want to see your face while you're inside me."

Oh yes. Chance kicked his shorts off his legs and added them to the pile of clothes jumbled on the floor. Soon they were both lying next to each other in only their underwear. "Red looks good on you," Chance said, pressing kisses on Luke's navel, just above his belly button.

Luke laughed, his flat stomach muscles contracting under Chance's lips. "I'm so glad to hear that." His legs spread wider as Chance slid between them, and his hand rested in Chance's hair. "You have no idea how long I've thought about this."

Chance looked up. Luke's eyes were dark with need and hunger. "About us?" he asked, scratching lightly on Luke's thigh muscle.

Luke nodded. "You and me, what it would be like to touch you. To taste you."

Chance's mouth pressed against Luke's cloth-covered cock, and he rubbed his nose against the damp spot. "I get to taste you first, babe." His fingers tugged the waistband down slowly, and he gasped softly when Luke's thick cock bobbed out of his underwear. Chance pulled the briefs down past Luke's knees and grasped the base of his cock, groaning at the feel of that hot, hard shaft. It had been a long time since he'd been this close to a cock that wasn't his own, and for a moment that fear overtook him—maybe he'd fuck this up.

Then Luke's fingers threaded softly through his hair, the gentlest scratches against his scalp. "You're so fucking beautiful, you know that?" Chance looked up—Luke didn't cuss often; in fact, Chance didn't think he'd ever heard him say any swear words. But those words gave Chance that small courage he needed, as he pressed soft kisses against Luke's shaft.

Luke's throaty groans filled their hotel room as Chance wrapped his lips around the head of Luke's cock and slid down, taking in as much as he could. Chance dragged his tongue along that thick vein under Luke's dick. His own cock ached listening to Luke's sounds of pleasure, but it only spurred Chance on. Over and over, his fist gripped that thick shaft and he went as deep as he could, until he felt those coarse hairs tickling his nose.

But Luke wanted to come when Chance was inside him, so he pulled off, pressing a biting kiss onto Luke's thigh as he rolled over onto the side of the bed. He'd dropped a small bag there earlier, and now he reached for into it and pulled out a bottle of lube and a condom.

Chance looked up. Luke's entire face and chest were flushed pink. His chest rose and fell with each deep breath, and when he spotted what Chance was doing, his hazel eyes widened. But he spread his legs further apart, pulling up one knee as Chance slid back into place. "Tell me if something doesn't feel—" he began, but then Luke's hands were on his head again, and their eyes met.

Nothing was wrong. How could anything be wrong, as long as they had each other?

Chance opened the lube and slicked two fingers, then poured a few drops between the cleavage of Luke's ass. His finger circled gently, the softest pressure against that tight hole and Chance pushed that finger inside Luke just as he took Luke's cock into his mouth again.

One finger, then the second slid inside Luke, opening his tight passage as Luke rocked against him, his cock thrusting shallowly into Chance's mouth and then back against his fingers. Chance hadn't ever seen anything so erotic as the way Luke took what he wanted from Chance. Just then Luke's hand tightened in Chance's hair and held his head right against Luke's groin. "Fuck—fuck, Chance, ahh..."

Chance stilled, closing his watering eyes as Luke's cock filled his mouth and he felt that pulse hit his throat. God. It was like porn, only it was happening to him. Luke's groans filled their room as his fingers loosened their grip. "Oh God..."

Chance lifted his head and caught Luke's eyes. "Hey, you okay?" Luke had wanted to come while Chance was inside him, and now that wasn't happening. He kissed Luke's thigh. "I'm sorry, babe."

But Luke just laughed. Sitting up, he leaned against an elbow and hung his head down as he grinned lazily. "Seriously, Chance, do I look like I'm complaining? That was incredible." Luke pulled Chance toward him and into a deep kiss, as if he were chasing his taste inside Chance's mouth. They fell backward onto the bed, and Luke's legs wrapped around Chance's hips. "You're amazing, but I'll have to do better next time."

Next time. But first, they had tonight, and they weren't done. Chance reached blindly for that condom he'd dropped next to the bed and pulled back from Luke's mouth. He tore the foil, trying not to remember how long it had been since he'd done this—*years*—and carefully rolled the condom onto his aching cock.

One more shift of his body, and Chance pressed his blunt knob against Luke's hole. Closing his eyes, he pushed slowly inside, the head of his cock breaching that softened muscle and then it was all heat, tight warmth pulling him deeper, drawing him inside Luke's body.

When Chance opened his eyes, Luke was staring at him. His hand slid behind Chance's neck and pulled him down into a blazing kiss as Chance's hips pumped in and out, and they found that sweet rhythm. Slow thrusts at first, almost leisurely, as Chance dragged this out as long as he could, despite Luke's gyrations underneath his body.

But Chance couldn't hold off forever, that heat licking at his belly as desire pooled inside him. *I want to feel you tomorrow.* His hips bucked harder, and Luke groaned. Once more, and again and again, until Chance leaned back, almost kneeling as he pulled Luke up with him, and wrapped Luke's legs around him. He thrust hard and deep, his own head hanging back and his hips pumping fast into Luke until he lost control and emptied himself into that tight tunnel.

Luke's eyes never left his, as Chance dropped his legs and fell forward. "Fuck. Oh God, that was amazing," he whispered. Luke's arms slid around him and held him as he came down from that orgasm.

"You were perfect," Luke whispered, and groaned quietly as Chance slipped out of him. "Better than I imagined."

It took a moment for Chance to speak again—had it really been that long since he'd done this? It felt so much more intense than he remembered, his emotions even stronger. Or maybe it was just because it was Luke, who hadn't stopped touching and kissing him. Chance rolled over to his side and pulled off the condom, then turned back toward Luke, and curled into his embrace. "I haven't—I mean, you—you're—" Too many words and none of them the right ones, so Chance just kissed him again. "I'm glad you're here with me."

Chapter Nineteen

They woke up late on Saturday, shared a sexy shower, and headed downstairs for the hotel's breakfast buffet. Luke overheard Chance's phone call with his aunt that morning; he thanked her for making golfing and lunch reservations for them, but he had other appointments and would see her that evening.

They spent most of the day sitting around the resort's pool. They talked more about their families and their past relationships—or lack of them, and their plans for the future, their hopes and dreams.

A smiling server kept bringing fresh drinks; the hotel special was a sparkling peach Bellini that Luke found ridiculously tasty. It was the most relaxing day he'd had in as long as he could remember.

Chance and Luke were on their way back to their hotel room when someone called out, "Cricket!"

Chance stopped and turned, and a wide smile broke out across his face as a young woman approached them, tall and slender, with a warm brown complexion and dazzling smile. "Rosie Posie," he said, and hugged her tight, lifting her off the ground. "I didn't think you'd make it."

She pulled back and kissed his cheek. "I hadn't planned on it, but then I heard you brought someone with you to shake the old people up. I would never let you have all the fun messing with the hive mind by yourself."

Chance turned back to Luke. "This is Roslyn McKinney. She might be my favorite cousin."

Roslyn punched his shoulder. "Might be?" Then she grinned at Luke. "The black sheep—well, the *biracial*-sheep of the family, if you will."

"Oh, that's a good one," Chance said with a groaning laugh.

"But I'm right. Either is equally damning to the aunties and a fair few uncles," Roslyn said.

Chance rolled his eyes but couldn't stop smiling. "Are you staying here or at the Marriott with everyone else?"

She wrapped her hand around Chance's arm. "As a matter of fact, I am staying here. This is a much better hotel, and I didn't want to embarrass Amanda any more than necessary—at least, not without a good reason and a sizable crowd to watch." She nodded toward the hotel bar, where a man sat at a piano, playing for tips. "Shall we get a quick drink before we gird our loins and meet the lions?"

Luke's face wrinkled in bewilderment at everything Roslyn said.

Or maybe it was the Bellinis.

"She exaggerates," Chance told him as they followed Roslyn to a small table close to the bar. "But, yeah, I guess we've always been the outsiders, haven't we?"

She nodded as a waitress listed the happy hour specials and took their orders. "In a family of lily-white blondes, I stand out. And then Cricket here—"

Luke interrupted. "I'm sorry. Can you explain that? Cricket?" he asked with a soft smile.

"She doesn't need to—" Chance began, only to be shushed by Roslyn.

"When we were little, Chance used to make these high-pitched chirping noises when he got excited about something." Her dark eyes gleamed at Luke. "Tell me, does he still do that?"

"Yes," Luke answered at the same time Chance said, "Enough about that." Then they all laughed, and Chance asked, "How's your mother doing?"

Roslyn shrugged. "She just accepted a vice-presidency in The Company." But Roslyn's voice couldn't hide her disappointment in that good news. "I know she'd be happier not working with everyone, but in the end, she couldn't say no to the money." She turned to Luke. "Now tell me all about you, so I can feel superior tonight, knowing things that the others won't know."

Luke explained about his work programming mobile apps, and Roslyn's eyes widened. "That sounds fascinating and yet, also dull as dirt." Her phone went off, and she made a soft gasp. "Time to run. But I'll see you both tonight." She finished her drink in one swallow and took Chance's hand. "We need to get together more often, Cricket. I miss your face. Luke, it was amazing meeting you."

"Miss you too," Chance replied, and they watched her head off toward the elevator.

"She's—" Luke began, but stopped, struggling for the word.

"Insane?" Chance said.

But Luke shook his head. "Effervescent. Like a bubble, floating around and making people smile." He grinned and finished his drink. "My mom was like that." Maybe that's why he instantly liked her.

Chance stood and reached his hands down to help Luke stand. "We should probably go too. I need another shower."

Luke's face went pink as he followed Chance to the elevators. "It's going to be hard to top the one we had this morning."

· · • • · • · • · ·

An hour and a half later, as Chance pulled his vehicle up to the gated entrance of his grandmother's neighborhood, a white-haired security guard stepped forward. Chance gave his name and mentioned the party and thanked the man when he raised the barrier to let them through. "I think he's been working at that gate since I was little," Chance said, and reached for Luke's hand as they turned down the street.

"She's been here for a long time?" Luke asked, taking in the neighborhood. Huge mansions, all of them just off the bay, with boats tied to their private piers behind the houses. "This is amazing."

"It was a great place to visit as a kid. My granddad would take me out in his boat, and we'd fish all day."

They pulled up to an enormous house, large and white, its architectural façade straight out of Cape Cod. Valets, dressed all in black, stood in front of the dwelling and took the Tahoe keys from Chance. Luke opened the back door and pulled out a gift bag, and then they headed up the long staircase into the mansion. "You ready?" Chance asked.

Luke nodded. "How about you?"

Chance sighed. "I should visit her more, and not wait for big gatherings like this to see her."

More than anything, Luke wanted to take Chance's hand and walk in, offering quiet strength for what had to be a difficult evening for Chance. Maybe he'd find the courage to do that as the evening progressed. "Let's do this so we can get back to our room," Luke said.

Chance nodded and caught Luke's eye. They'd get through this.

One more deep breath, and they walked through the oversized front door, and Luke's eyes widened. The house was filled to the brim with people in fancy dress, talking loudly and hugging each other. "This isn't fifty people," Luke whispered in his ear.

"It's not." Easily three times that, and probably more, Chance realized, and exhaled loud as the first of the cousins approached him, then another, and soon he and Luke were surrounded by his extended family. Chance did his best to point out his aunts and uncles, but Luke was quickly overwhelmed with names and faces. "Has anyone seen my parents?" Chance asked.

One of Chance's cousins—it was hard to tell them apart, as they all had long blonde hair and thin lips—pointed a sharp red fingernail at the back of the house. "I think they're on the veranda." She spoke to Chance, but Luke felt those eyes bore into him. Just at that moment, another woman called out to them. "Chance, your mother wants to see you. She said that it's important."

Chance turned to Luke. He rested his hand on Luke's arm. "Let me go see what's up, and find where my grandmother is, okay? I'll be right back." He pointed at the bar, off in the corner. "Get yourself a drink, and I'll come get you in a minute and give you the grand tour."

Get yourself a drink, Luke thought to himself. After all that he'd had at the hotel, that was the last thing he needed. But he walked toward the bar, unsurprised when he saw how well it was stocked and all of it free. He asked the perky young woman tending the bar for a bottle of water and thanked her when she handed it to him.

Luke turned in the direction Chance had gone, but there was no sign of him. The sun was going down, so he headed to the outside deck and found a spot close to the pier and watched the light bouncing off the water. The view was stunning, and he imagined a small blond boy playing here, running up and down the large deck with his toys.

"Are you okay?"

Luke jumped at the small touch on his shoulder. "What—"

Roslyn stepped back, worried. "Oh hey, I'm sorry. We met earlier, remember? Roslyn?" She looked different, her curls loose and cascading down her back, and a crisp white sundress that accentuated her mocha skin. "I didn't mean to startle you."

"No, don't apologize. I remember." Luke closed his eyes. *Couldn't he be normal once, just for one day?"* I was lost in thought." He returned her warm smile. "Are you having fun?" he asked.

Roslyn snorted and leaned her crossed arms against the tall deck railing. "About as much as you are. I appreciate the sentiment of family keeping in touch, but I can count the number of people here that I want to talk to on one hand." She turned to face him. "The real question is, how are you doing? Are you having fun?" she asked, but her cheeky grin announced that she already knew the answer to that. "Where did Chance go? He abandoned you already, the asshole."

It took Luke a moment, but he understood she was joking. "His parents wanted to talk to him about something. He said it wouldn't be long." Roslyn's brow arched at that. "Please tell me, is there anything that I need to know before I meet his parents or his grandmother? I don't want to go in and embarrass myself or Chance."

Roslyn grinned. "Aw. You're as adorable as Chance said you were." Her sympathetic expression was tinged with wariness. "I'm afraid there's few people here who are happy to see you. Chance's parents have ignored his sexual preference for years, and they've been able to because he doesn't date often and *never* brings anyone around. There's no one here closer to Chance than I am, and you're the first boyfriend that I've met since he was in college."

That pit of worry in Luke's stomach twisted as Roslyn spoke. "But they know who I am."

"Oh yes, Chance told them all that he was bringing you." Her face hardened. "I just hope he did it for the right reason."

What would the wrong reason be? But before Luke could ask, another woman approached them. "Roz, it's been a long time." She found space on the railing next to Roslyn, her straight blond hair accentuating the sharp cheekbones and deeply arched brows. "And you must be Luke. I'm Charlotte." She extended her hand, her arm covered in gold bangles that matched the many rings on her hands. "Chance has told us all about you."

Warning signs went off in Luke's head. Where Roslyn had been warm and friendly in her introduction, Charlotte's approach was more like a lion checking out a lame gazelle, sizing it up for lunch. "Hello Charlotte. Are you a cousin?" he asked as he shook her hand.

She smiled and showed off her perfect white teeth. "Sort of—you know, the families are all connected in one way or another. But no, I'm not a blood relation—thank goodness, right?" Roslyn rolled her eyes, but Charlotte continued. "I just wanted to come and meet the man who's got Chance's head turned all around right now. You seem like a nice guy, sugar. Just be careful. Don't let him lead you on."

"Go away." Roslyn nudged her with her stiletto heel. "I don't want people to think we're friends. It will ruin my street cred." Charlotte winked at Luke, then walked back to the larger crowd. Roslyn didn't take her eyes off Charlotte until she was out of sight. "Be careful of that one. She's invested in your unhappiness."

Luke was confused. "Who is she? What did she mean about not being a real cousin?"

"She's a snake, and not even hiding her fangs tonight." Roslyn started to speak but looked around. More people had joined them, so she reached for Luke's hand. "Come with me. I know a place we can talk in private."

She led him down through the main room, filled with even more people than had been there thirty minutes prior when they arrived. Down a side hallway and through a door, and they ended up underneath an enormous staircase that led to the bedrooms upstairs.

Despite being hidden away, the wall had thick lattice panels, and they could still see many of the guests wandering in and out of the main room. "Chance and I used to play here and overhear what people were talking about." She pointed out one of Chance's aunts. "That's Amanda. The woman she's talking to is Jayne, who's my mom. She married a black man, and had me," Roz pointed at herself. "But they divorced a few years ago, and the family has almost forgiven her, except when they see me."

"That's awful," Luke whispered.

Roz shrugged. "I exaggerate. Most people don't care, but those that do are particularly nasty, and unfortunately, they are the ones who are vying the hardest for control of Nanna's money. Okay, see the woman who just joined them? That is the snake's mother, Kendra Foxworthy. Her family owns some refineries down the coast. She and Chance's mom have planned Chance and Charlotte's wedding since they were toddlers. It's ridiculous, plotting like we're some feudal kingdoms who want to merge our ancestral lands. It's medieval. If Edwards Oil truly wanted to acquire Foxworthy Petroleum, then they'd do a stock buyout, like proper pirates." She grinned at her own words. "Anyway, a few of the harpies are still holding on to the hopes that Chance will grow up and return to the fold while Charlotte's still young enough to pop out an heir, so they can forgive him for this little gay phase."

Luke's mind spun at all of this. An arranged marriage? "They all sound horrible, all of them. I don't understand why he wants to be close to any of them at all."

Roz's face fell. "Like I said, it's not everyone. Some of the cousins our age are actually pretty cool. Chance doesn't know that because he doesn't give them the chance to get close. But the older family members—" She shook her head. "The only people he keeps in touch with are Nanna and me. I mean, he talks to his parents on the regular, but that's out of some sense of filial duty."

Just then, Luke heard Chance's voice coming from right above him. "It's a lot to think about," Chance said, his footsteps thudding on the stairs.

A woman's voice said, "Yes, dear, but I hope you'll give me the answer that I want. Consider it a birthday present."

Roslyn put her finger to her mouth. "That's Nanna," she whispered.

Luke froze, and cocked his ear up to hear better.

"Now, what's this I hear about you bringing a young man to my birthday party?" There was a long pause. "Tell me, how serious is this?"

Chance stammered. "Um, it's just—we're friends, really. Just friends, and we're getting to know each other. No more than that."

Another long silence. Then— "Friends, eh? Oh Chance..." Nanna's voice was dismissive as she walked down the stairs and toward the rest of the crowd.

"Nanna—wait." Chance scrambled after her, and soon they were out of earshot.

Luke couldn't move. *Just friends?* Is that what they were to each other? Luke understood the need for privacy more than anyone, and he prized his own independence. Seeing those qualities in Chance had been appealing.

But Luke also valued honesty, and right now all he saw was Chance casting him and their relationship aside to please his family. Maybe if they hadn't spent last night wrapped up in each other's arms, it might be easier to digest those words. *Didn't you know this was going to happen?* He was an idiot for coming here, for believing Chance wanted a future with him.

"Luke." Roslyn took his arm, and snapped him out of his daze. "Hey, look, I don't think he meant—" But her face showed the same confusion, the same... disappointment. "Let me go get him so you can talk."

"That's okay. It doesn't matter what he meant." *Actions speak louder than words, right?* Luke ran a hand through his hair. "I just—I thought we—" Doesn't matter now what Luke thought. "It was nice meeting you, Roslyn. Thank you for being so kind to me and take care of yourself."

"Luke—" Roslyn called out, but Luke headed back through the corridors the way they came. Once he was back in the main hall, he spotted the front door and walked out as fast as he could go.

People were still showing up for the party. A couple stepped out of their Tesla and frowned as Luke stumbled past them down the long stairs that led toward the street. But where was he going to go now? Stranded in another town, an hour from home, with no vehicle.

His hand slid into his pants pocket and wrapped around his hotel key card. *It's a start.* Luke jogged down past the entrance to the gated community and pulled out his phone and opened the Uber app.

The sooner he was back at the hotel, the better.

A few minutes later, Luke was packed and heading down to the elevator. Did he have a plan? No, just a head full of sad, confused thoughts. *He'll come back here for you. He didn't mean it. Don't leave yet.* But Luke pushed that voice aside.

He got a text message just as he exited the hotel's entrance, dragging Jessica's purple luggage next to him.

> Chance: *Where are you? I'm in my car. Tell me where you're at and I can come get you.*
> Chance: *I'm sorry. Please let me explain.*

Luke stared at it for a moment, then pocketed his phone and walked along the long seawall promenade until he found a spot to sit and watch the water.

Kids ran around with sparklers, and he heard a few firecrackers going off in the distance. *That's right, it's the Fourth of July.* It was just getting dark when his phone rang. Should he answer? Wouldn't it be better to just end things right now?

But when he lifted the phone, it wasn't Chance's number that appeared on his screen.

It was Maggie, Jessica's friend from the rescue.

He answered immediately. "What happened?" he asked, his heart twisted in apprehension.

Maggie didn't waste any time. "She got arrested for trespassing. Houston PD picked her up after someone complained about her trespassing on their property. But she had bolt cutters on her, so they added breaking and entering to the charge."

Of course. "Give me the address, and I'll be there in an hour." Luke looked at his watch. "Maybe a little longer. Will she need a bond?"

"I don't know. I can find out." Maggie sounded scared.

Luke scrubbed his face and looked around. Would it be cheaper to rent a car or Uber from one town to the other? Luke pulled out his app and put his home in as a destination, surprised when he saw someone quickly pick up his request and head his way.

At least this one thing went his way tonight.

As Luke walked toward the main boulevard, some of that ugly tension from the evening fell off his shoulders. Jessica needed him, even if Chance didn't.

A small red Toyota Civic pulled up alongside him. Luke double checked the license plate and driver's face against the information on the app. "Good evening, Benito," he said, and stepped into the backseat with his luggage.

Benito waved at him, then went back to driving.

It took a little over an hour to get home. During the entire trip, fireworks burst all over the city. Luke watched from the back of the Toyota and wondered where Chance was, and why today had all gone wrong.

Chapter Twenty

"What do you mean, he left?" Chance stood in a hallway just off the kitchen, after having spent the previous twenty minutes storming through the house looking for Luke, before Roslyn pulled him into the corridor.

"Will you settle down? They're going to throw you out on your ass if you don't stop yelling at people—including me."

Chance growled loudly and tried to stay out of the way of the steady stream of servers walking in and out of the kitchen, carrying trays of canapes and champagne as he questioned Roslyn. "Okay, okay. I just don't understand. Where did he go?" he asked, frustrated.

"I told you—I don't know." Her crossed arms and stern expression were so uncharacteristic of his free-spirit cousin that Chance knew immediately something bad had happened. "We were next to the staircase, hiding out in that special spot. You know which one I'm talking about."

Chance knew. It was a great hiding place if you didn't want to be found, or if you wanted to hear something without anyone knowing. "Okay, you were hiding. I get that. It was a dick move for me to bring him to the party and then just leave him, but I needed to make sure my parents weren't going to be assholes to him. Then I was summoned by Nanna, and before I knew it—" Chance waved his hand in the air, nearly hitting a server. "I didn't mean to leave him so long."

"You didn't think that letting your parents know he was coming was something you should have done before you got to the party?" Roslyn asked him.

Chance closed his eyes. "They knew, but..." Chance had screwed up this introduction to the family. "They knew I was bringing a man, but I should have made them aware that I would not tolerate them disrespecting Luke. Clearly mistakes were made."

Roslyn snorted. "You don't know the half of it."

"Please enlighten me. Who did Luke overhear?" Was it his parents? Maybe some nasty cousins?

"As a matter of fact, it was you. You and Nanna were standing right above us. Do you remember what you told her when she asked you about the young man you brought with you tonight?"

Chance closed his eyes. Yes, he recalled the conversation.

"Tell me, how serious is this?"

"Um, it's just—we're friends, really. Just friends, and we're getting to know each other. No more than that."

"Okay. Okay," Chance repeated. "Luke overheard Nanna ask me who he was, and I said that he was a friend."

"Just a friend," Roslyn added. "That's what really drove the knife in the back, if you want my opinion." She quieted for a long moment, and tried to catch Chance's eyes, but he closed them, shut tight as if he could rewind time and go back to that moment. Finally, he opened his eyes when she reached down and took his hand. "Chance, why did you say it like that? Is that how you think of him? Does he think that you two are further along in your relationship than you do?"

Chance leaned his head back against the wall and stared blankly in front of him. "I don't know why I said it. I guess—when I got here and told my parents that Luke was with me, they didn't say anything. Whatever was happening with Nanna, that was more important than chiding me about my date for the birthday party. Dad told me that Nanna had asked to see me as soon as I arrived, and everyone rushed me up the stairs."

"What was so important that Nanna wanted to see you when you got here?" Roz asked. After getting a few more side-eye glances from the servers, she took his hand again. "Let's get out of here."

He followed her to another private spot they knew, walking too fast for anyone to stop them. They landed in a private corner of the upper deck overlooking the water. "Okay, now spill it. What was going on with Nanna?"

"She asked me if I was ready to take more responsibility with the charitable foundation. She said she wants to make some changes, important changes, and she doesn't trust the aunts and uncles to make the changes that she wants to make. They're ignoring her wishes." Chance sighed and rubbed his eyes. "Don't tell anyone. I don't know how much of this is real or how much is just her being mad at the foundation's board of directors and venting to me. But then, as we were heading downstairs, she asked about who I brought, and—" Chance shook his head. "She seemed upset about it, like she was angry that I'd brought a 'young man' with me. It shocked me, I guess, but her tone and I... I panicked."

We're friends. Just friends. No more than that. Chance groaned as he recalled those words.

Roslyn's face fell. "I'm sorry, Chance, but from where we were standing, it did sound as if she was upset about something, and you said—well, you said what you said, and we both heard it. Luke's eyes went wide, and he got the fuck out of here as fast as he could."

"But why was she upset?" Chance didn't understand why his Nanna, who'd always been supportive to him his whole life, why she was angry today? "I didn't mean to ruin her party or make her mad. I thought bringing Luke was a good idea."

"Did you?" Roslyn aimed her gaze squarely at him. "Yes, the whole family knows that you're gay, but have you ever brought anyone to any of our family functions with you? Have you talked to anyone about your love life, or included any of us in any of your personal activities, all those charities that keep you so busy? You're locked up tighter than a safe, Cricket. I know more about you than maybe anyone here, and I still only get to see you a couple times a year, tops." She twirled a long curl around her finger. "For someone who's out of the closet, you don't act like it."

Chance didn't know how to respond. *Was she right?* I guess I've always been afraid how people would react."

"But you never gave anyone a chance. Can you imagine how good it would be for those aunties and uncles and cousins to see you with someone in a happy and loving relationship? And you know damn well you're not the only gay cousin. There are a few grandkids out there that want to come out or let some of the others know about their sexual preferences. But if Chance, the darling favorite of the family, if he's too scared to bring his boyfriend around, then what does that tell the younger ones?"

Chance put his hands up. "Wait a minute. I'm not some poster boy spokesman for gay people."

Roz snorted. "In this family, you are, and you're a terrible one." They stared at each other until she reached out and hugged him tight. "I want to talk about this more, and I really want to know what you told Nanna about the foundation, holy shit, and most of all, I want to spend time with you, and not just when we're obliged to be in the same room together." She pulled back. "But right now, you need to go find Luke and tell him you're sorry."

Chance nodded. "Why don't we hang out more?"

She laughed. "You're always so busy," she said, making air quotes on that last word. "Go. I'll make excuses for you with *la familia*."

Chance kissed her cheek and then headed down a back staircase that few people knew.

He pulled out his phone to send Luke a text and froze. His screen was black. He pressed the power button and growled at the sight of a large red battery flashing.

Of course. He'd been out at the pool with Luke, taking pictures and listening to music. He never thought about needing to charge his phone. *Fuck!*

Chance ran down the steps, almost tripping into the valets, who hadn't expected anyone to be leaving so soon. After he retrieved his Tahoe and keys, Chance threw the phone on the charger, and as soon as it turned on, he shot off two quick texts and sped toward the hotel.

Chance: *Where are you? I'm in my car. Tell me where you're at and I can come get you.*
Chance: *I'm sorry. Please let me explain.*

Had he hit every red light in Galveston on the way to the hotel? It felt like it, and after he parked, he rushed through the lobby, pacing as he waited for an elevator.

But the moment he opened the door to their hotel room, he froze in place.

Luke's key card was lying on the desk.

He walked into the bedroom and sighed. Luke's suitcase and clothes were gone.

Luke was gone.

Chapter Twenty-one

Jessica was already in the kitchen when Luke went down to make some breakfast. She sat at the table, still in her pajamas, reading something from her phone. "Good morning," he said to her, and reached into the pantry. He pulled out two packets of maple and brown sugar instant oatmeal and emptied them into a bowl while he heated water in the microwave. Next was the coffee—where was his favorite mug? "Are you okay?" he asked when she didn't respond.

"I'm okay." Neither of them had a full night of sleep. Luke had arrived back in Houston close to midnight. He made it to the county jail and secured Jessica's release with a bond and they got home just before three AM. "Thanks again for helping me last night."

"You're welcome," he said, and yawned loudly as he walked back to the table.

Jessica set her phone down and stood. She walked to the fridge and pulled out a carton of eggs and a package of bacon. "Are you going to tell me what happened with Chance?" she asked as she set a pan on top of the stove.

Luke rolled his eyes and took a sip of his coffee. "Are you going to tell me about the bolt cutters?"

She didn't answer. Then… "I will if you will."

That was fair. Luke poured the hot water into his oatmeal and stirred slowly. "If I understood it myself, perhaps I'd be able to. But I'm still confused by it all, my own actions in particular."

Jessica nodded in understanding. "Something must have triggered you, Luke, if you left the party without him." She opened the bacon and threw a few slices into the pan. "I feel bad, though—like, maybe you would've stayed and talked to him last night if I hadn't gotten into trouble. I didn't mean for you to come home like that."

Luke rested his chin on his hand as he recalled the previous night, and how fast it all happened. "I couldn't have spoken to him yesterday about this. I was too angry; still am, I think." He bit his lip. "The question is, why am I so angry? When I think about it, this pain flares inside me, but honestly, what he said wasn't that terrible." Luke lifted his head toward Jessica. "Chance and I have gone on a handful of dates, that's all. We've made no promises to each other, said nothing that should even be construed as a relationship. We're friends," Luke said, repeating Chance's words.

"Then why did that hurt you?" Jessica asked, pushing her bacon around in the skillet.

Luke shrugged. "That's what I've been asking myself all morning. Why did it hurt so much, hearing him say that?"

Jessica added some eggs to the hot skillet. "I know you've only been on a couple dates, but you've been half in love with Chance Edwards for a long time. And—" Jessica hesitated. She bit her lip as her eyes rested on Luke. "You don't get close to people. I mean, I don't either, so I'm not saying it's wrong, but we don't let humans into our space, you know? And we haven't since the accident."

The accident, that unspoken wound that still cast a pall over this house. He nodded. "I miss them every day."

"Me too." Jessica sniffled and touched her eyes with her finger. "But you let this one in, and you got hurt."

He took a few bites of his oatmeal in silence. "What is in a Bellini?"

Jessica finished cooking her eggs and slid them on a plate with the bacon. "Prosecco and peaches, I think." Luke sighed. "And are you planning on seeing him again?" she asked as she sat at the table next to him.

Luke shook his head. "I don't think so. We both behaved badly."

They stayed quiet, both in their thoughts. When Luke finished his oatmeal, he set the empty dish in the sink. "So, what's going to happen to you?" he asked. "Do you have to go to court?"

Jessica's face fell, and she blew out a long breath. "I've got to figure out what to do about this charge. Maggie talked to someone at the rescue who seems to think that I might be able to plead down to a misdemeanor if I can make a case for our actions. That we were trying to rescue these dogs, not steal them. That they were in imminent danger. I don't know." The morose expression on her face wasn't a look Luke saw often on his sister. "But it was fucking scary last night, even before the cops showed up. I thought we might get shot." She picked up a piece of bacon and chewed it. "I'd never felt like that before."

Luke's panic set in, though he kept it under control as best he could. His voice wavered. "You can't be doing this anymore, not with a criminal charge looming over your head. Even if you can get the charge reduced, they won't be so lenient if there's a second occurrence."

Jessica began to cry, and tears streamed down her face. "This is my whole life, Luke. What else am I supposed to do?" Her fists balled up at her sides. "Why is every day such a battle?"

He didn't know how to support her other than just being here for his sister. "We will figure out something. There are many ways to help the dogs. You do so much for them, Jessica, but you won't be helping them if you're in jail." That seemed to get through to her, and she nodded. "How is Sadie?" Luke asked.

Jess wiped her face with her napkin. "Oh, good news there. We've got someone who wants her. I was supposed to go over today for a house visit, but—" Jessica shrugged. "I feel worthless right now, like I just want to climb back in bed until I figure out what to do with my life."

Luke's brows furrowed. "Might I suggest you do that after you do the home visit? One, you might feel low at the moment, but Sadie's needs are important as well and can't be discounted just because you messed up your life. Two—" Luke said, counting off on his fingers as Jessica watched, "—it is my belief that helping Sadie find a forever home will raise your lagging spirits."

"You're probably right." Jessica walked over and hugged Luke, who wrapped an arm around her in return. "But what about you? What's going to raise your lagging spirits?" she asked and pushed a stray tendril from his forehead.

Luke wrinkled his nose. "That remains to be seen."

"You won't feel better until you've spoken to him," she told him.

"Unfortunately." Luke made a face when Jess messed his hair before leaving the room.

But the last thing that Luke wanted to do right now was face Chance.

Chapter Twenty-two

Chance had neglected to close the curtains to his hotel room the previous evening when he dropped into his bed, angry and a little intoxicated, so the sun shone bright on his face as it rose around half-past six in the morning. His eyes fluttered a few times before he rolled over, pulling a pillow over his head, and cursing the bright light.

Luke had just spent one night in the hotel—and yet, the pillow smelled like him. That anger that had welled up quick subsided now, as he remembered the party, and how Luke left him there alone.

Fuck. Well, it wasn't like he could get back to sleep now. Chance reached for his phone and chuckled bitterly at the nineteen missed messages, though none from Luke—six from his mother, five from Roz, two from Charlotte, a few more from assorted family that he'd ignored or yelled at while trying to find his boyfriend. The final one was from his grandmother. *Please join me for breakfast this morning. 9:00 at my house. Bring your friend.*

He ignored all but that last one.

Chance had no intentions of returning to the hotel after his breakfast with Nanna, so he packed everything up and threw his bag in the backseat of his Tahoe. A shower and shave had him looking presentable, even if he still felt miserable inside. There was so much that Chance still didn't understand, so he didn't blame Luke for leaving.

Right now, Chance was disappointed in himself.

The ride to his grandmother's house was just as beautiful in the morning, the sun bouncing off the water. The valets were gone, all signs of the party poofed away like Cinderella's pumpkin. Chance parked in the long driveway and headed up the steps toward her front door.

An older woman answered the door, so thin that a good stiff wind could knock her over. "Good morning, Chance."

"Hi, Aunt Libby." Chance stepped close and kissed her ruddy cheek. "I didn't see you last night."

"And yet, I saw you." Aunt Libby wasn't really his aunt, but a friend of the family who moved in with his grandmother after the death of her husband years and years ago, and now acted as a companion to his Nanna. "That was quite the shitstorm, sweetie."

Chance sighed. "I'm sorry about that."

Libby snorted. "I daresay there's plenty of blame to go around," she said and led him through the house to the large wooden deck in the back. "Toast or biscuits?"

"Biscuits if you made them," Chance said. Libby beamed as she walked toward the kitchen. He took a deep breath and walked through the back door to where his grandmother sat, straight-backed, her eyes on the boats passing in and out of the bay. "Good morning, Nanna."

"Good morning, Chance." Evelyn Brightwell Edwards turned to him and offered her bony hand, which he held as he sat down at the table next to her. Her blue eyes were clear and sharp, even at eighty, as she glanced behind him. "Are you alone this morning?"

"Yes."

"Where is he?"

Straight the point, that was his grandmother. "Um, he left last night and went home. Something came up, I guess, and he couldn't stay."

She turned back toward the gulf. "Once when you were seven, you took a box of cookies from the pantry, and when I asked you if you knew what happened to them, you pretended you didn't know what I meant. That was, until last evening, the last time you told me an untruth." Libby stepped back out with fresh coffee, refilling Nanna's mug and pouring a cup for Chance before setting the pot down on the deck and returning inside. "All I can drink is decaf now, I hope you don't mind."

"It's not a problem." Chance felt like he was seven again, being scolded for lying. "I just didn't want to disrupt the party."

"Didn't you, Chance? If not, why did you bring your boyfriend? That's who he is, isn't he?" Her voice grew louder as she spoke, and a few seagulls who'd landed on the wooden deck railing took flight.

A few seconds passed before Chance answered. "I wanted him to be. But I don't know what's going on now."

"Well, Roslyn is the best source of information in this family, and she told me that Luke—that's his name, yes? She said that you brought this young man to the party to stick it to your mother, but later Luke heard you say that you two were just friends, and that hearing that hurt his feelings and he left. Is that correct?"

This must be what cross-examination felt like. "That's what happened." Chance said in a low voice. "I shouldn't have brought him to get back at my mom. I was just so angry, you know?"

"Chance, I've known your mother a lot longer than you, and I understand completely." Her laugh was low and rumbling. "But what I still can't understand is why, after going to all that trouble, why you pretended he wasn't your beau? Why didn't you bring him to me and let me meet him? Why did you call him 'your friend'?"

Chance set his coffee mug down. "I think—once we got to the party, and I saw everyone, I realized I'd made a mistake. Not that it embarrassed me to be with Luke, but it was too soon to do the whole family thing. We haven't been dating long, and he doesn't like crowds. But he came because I asked him." The full weight of Chance's mistake punched him in the gut.

"And then you abandoned him in a room full of sharks," Nanna added.

Chance's stomach twisted in a knot. "And then I lied to you. Not that I meant to be untruthful. I just didn't want you to be mad at me."

Nanna sat back in her chair and took another sip from her coffee. Her eyes drifted back to the water. "There's a box over on that chair. Pick it up, won't you, and bring it to me?" Chance reached out and picked up the small wooden box, about the size of a shoe box. It had intricate wooden carvings and looked old. "Open it."

He did, and found a photograph on top, a young man with golden hair and a bright smile standing next to a horse, and another photograph of the same man in a military uniform. A bundle of letters tied with twine were under the pictures, along with a plastic bag filled with military medals. "Who is this?" he asked.

"That's Travis. He was my baby brother." Evelyn took a shaky breath. "He was the light of my life growing up, and we were the best of friends. You know I married into all this money. I wasn't born with the Edwards silver spoon in my mouth. Travis and I grew up on a small horse ranch near Laredo. And we had no secrets from each other."

Her eyes filled with tears. "What happened to him?" Chance asked.

"It was different back then," Evelyn began, and reached for the photograph of Travis and the horse. "Not that it's easy for you and your friends, your community. But Travis, he had to keep it all a secret. He fell in love with a studious young man who moved to town and worked at the bank. No one could know, Chance. *No one*, not back then. It was illegal, and worse—it was not what good men did. Especially not according to my father."

Chance glanced down at the faded photographs of Travis in uniform and turned it over. Corporal Travis Brightwell, November 1, 1968. "Your brother joined the military?"

She nodded. "I had just gotten married and wasn't there to protect him from our father's wrath when he found out. He marched Travis down to the recruitment office in town and forced him to enlist that same day. Told him to come back a real man or not to come back at all." Her lips quivered, and she pressed them together. "They killed him near Da Nang soon after that photo was taken."

Chance's jaw dropped and didn't speak for a minute. "You've never told me about him."

"I never talked to anyone about Travis," Evelyn said in a low voice, but her eyes sparkled with moisture. "Your grandfather knew, of course, I couldn't keep anything from him. And I kept in touch with his young man for a few years, but I had young children and he moved back to Louisiana. I don't know what ever happened to him."

It was like a punch in the gut. "I'm sorry I was dishonest last night, Nanna. I thought you'd be mad at me."

"I am mad—because you didn't share this with me, Chance. Who you are and who you love is such a big part of your life, and knowing that you tried to hide something so important to you, that you didn't want me to know—well, that hurt my feelings. The whole family has tittle tattled about you for years, but you've never talked to me, or brought anyone to meet me. So, when I heard you finally had a sweetheart and were bringing him to my party, I was thrilled—until..."

"Until I lied to you," Chance murmured.

"Until you lied to yourself." Evelyn took Chance's hands in her own. "Be proud of who you are, my sweet boy, and be proud of who you love. Nothing would make this old lady happier than knowing that you had what my dear brother could not." A tear rolled down her cheek. "You've always been my favorite, that's no secret. But it's because you always reminded me so much of my Travis. He was beautiful inside and outside, just like you."

Chance's fear caused him to push people away, people who loved and cared about him. He saw that now. "How do I fix this?"

The older woman sighed. "You might not. I imagine it depends on how hurt your young man was by what he heard, and if you both feel that it's worth what it takes to repair that injury." Evelyn nodded at the door, where Libby stood inside, waiting.

She stepped out onto the deck and brought their breakfast plates—eggs, bacon, and biscuits with butter and jam. "Everything okay?" Libby asked and looked down at the box.

"We're having a splendid chat, thank you." Evelyn nodded as Libby left. "Chance, I hope you and Luke can mend your relationship, and I'm sorry I didn't get to meet him. Rosie said he made her laugh, and she's hard to impress."

They ate and talked about Chance's work at the clinic, and he told her about his involvement with the Pride Center and the dog rescue where Luke and his sister volunteered. Her eyes lit up as he spoke, and whenever they clouded over with moisture, he knew her brother was in her thoughts. "I tell you what, Nanna. I promise to always be open and honest with everyone that comes into my life from now on. No more hiding, ever. But I think you should take these out of this box and put them somewhere in this house for everyone to see."

She touched the medals as they jingled in the bag. "You're absolutely right, my sweet boy." She set the pictures up against her mug facing her and smiled at them. "Oh, he'd like you."

Chapter Twenty-three

It was turning out to be a hot July, and the temperature was almost eighty-five degrees at ten AM when Luke left the pet store with their weekly supply of dog food—only two bags of kibble this time, new chew toys, and some puppy supplements. With any luck, he wouldn't have to leave the house again today.

Luke didn't recognize the old Chevy truck parked in front of their house when he pulled into the driveway. Dog crates in the back meant they were most likely friends from the rescue, but Jessica had been lying low since her arrest—the looming court case worried her more than she wanted to admit. Her mood hadn't improved since the arrest and being stuck at home kept her cranky and sad. With any luck, Luke hoped, these friends would improve her mood.

He opened the garage door and tossed the bags of kibble into their normal spot and walked into the house through the kitchen. Voices from the living room caught his attention, and soon Jessica called his name.

He found them seated on the sofa, with Willie and Waylon, her latest fosters, sleeping at their feet. "This is my brother, Luke. Luke, this is Dani Reynolds. She works with End of the Rainbow Rescues."

Luke recognized the name and nodded at the older woman. "Ms. Reynolds."

"Dani, please. I'm pleased to meet you both." Dani Reynolds pushed a wayward strand of ash brown hair out of her warm gray eyes. "I was just telling your sister that we've been following her and her partners on social media for the last several months, and we're impressed with the lengths they've gone to trying to save those dogs in danger."

Jessica's face dropped. "I'm afraid I won't be doing much of that anymore." She wrung her hands on her lap. "I don't know if you know—"

Dani nodded. "I saw your post about that. I'm so sorry that happened. But I might be able to help."

Luke sat down, curious.

"First, let me tell you a little about our organization." She held up a canvas bag with a rainbow emblazoned across the front, a small dog paw at one end. "We're made up of volunteers, many of whom come from the LGBTQ community. Like many rescues, we've been working out of our homes for several years now, which is convenient in some ways, but limits our ability to appear as a legitimate charitable organization."

Jessica nodded in understanding. "If it wasn't for my social media accounts and ordinary people donating, I'm not sure how we'd be able to stay afloat without dipping into our personal savings."

Dani smiled. "Well, I'm happy to tell you we've had a recent donation to our rescue. A very, very generous benefactor has offered to help our organization—well, get more organized. We're planning on renting out a store front with office space to promote End of the Rainbow Rescues as a real charitable organization, create and sell merchandise, and get our name out there nationwide. Finding volunteers to drive our rescues to their new homes is our highest priority, and as we both know, it takes money to do all of this. With this donation, we'll be able to do that and still keep as much money as possible set aside for the animals."

"I'm thrilled for you," Jessica said, a wistful smile on her face. "But I'm still not sure why you've come here to see me."

"With this new office comes a lot more responsibilities. The rescue organizers, Roxanne and Ella, both have full-time jobs, as do I. As much as I'd love to retire and do this full time, I'm not quite there yet. But we have enough for a small stipend and are looking for someone to work as our office manager. It would be part-time at first—answering email, managing social media accounts, and helping us with transports. My son Noah has been helping to maintain the website for a few years but he's busier now too." She shook her head. "What I'm trying to say is that we respect what you've been doing, and you come highly recommended in the rescue community. If you and your organization would like to partner with us, we'd be honored and would love to put you on our pay-roll."

Jessica sat there a moment, stunned. "Jess, what do you think?" Luke asked.

She took a deep breath. "I think that I'd like to join your organization." She looked down at the sleeping dogs at her feet. "Whatever it takes to help find them good homes."

Dani's bright smile lit up her face. "That's fantastic. I'll be in touch once we get more information about the new office space, and when we can move in and set up." She stood. "It was nice to meet the both of you." She picked up her purse and halted. "I almost forgot—we've got a fundraiser going on at Briscoe Park this weekend, as part of their Pride in July celebration. One of my son's friends plays in a band and they'll be there with music. We'll have some of our fosters who are ready to be adopted there. We'd love to see you and your partners in rescue there. I can introduce you to the rest of our team. And please feel free bring any of your own foster animals that are ready for adoption."

Jessica nodded and walked Dani to the door, thanking her profusely. Once it was closed, she turned back to Luke. "Oh my God, what just happened?" Jessica ran over to hug Luke and threw her arms around him. "I can't believe that. A job in rescue, Luke, a real job. It's all I ever wanted. And they're legit, too. I've followed them for years and know all about their transporting. They go all over the country. And I know she said part-time at first but that's fine, it's perfect for me." She finally stopped talking and took a breath, then arched a brow when she spotted Luke's face. "What do you think? Not a good idea?" she asked.

Luke shrugged. "I don't know what to say. You are correct, it sounds good. It sounds perfect for you. This opportunity would allow you to stay involved without putting yourself in danger." The dogs both woke up at Jessica's chatter and ambled toward the dog door, letting themselves out. "You'll still be able to foster." He smiled at her. "Let's see how it goes."

But once he got upstairs, Luke settled in front of his computer and opened a browser. What was Dani's son's name? Oh yes. *Noah Reynolds End of the Rainbow.*

He clicked a few links and scrolled, but it took less than four minutes of searching before he found it. *Bingo.* Just as Luke suspected, the proof was there on their Instagram account. The picture was from the previous year, but it showed a group of young men all holding a dog leash and laughing. Chance even had his scrubs on, and the brightest smile on his face.

Chance had clearly organized this lifeline for Jessica. He'd gotten Dani Reynolds to come over and offer her a job because he knew what kind of trouble she was in, and how much she was hurting.

And he'd done it without either him or Jess knowing that he was behind it.

Luke sat back in his chair and folded his hands. His heart ached at the sight of Chance's smile, and he knew he'd never see it aimed at him like that again.

Chapter Twenty-four

That same week, Chance called his mother and asked her to meet him at a local coffeehouse close to his office. He didn't explain why he wanted to talk to her but assured her it was important. Chance arrived early and found a comfortable corner they could speak in, away from studying students and groups of friends laughing and chatting with each other.

When she entered, he waved her over. "Thanks for meeting with me," he said as he stood and kissed her cheek.

Marcia smiled at that gesture, but it didn't reach her eyes. "I don't suppose I had much choice. You were very close-lipped on the phone why you wanted to talk," she said as she sat down.

Chance signaled to the wait staff, and a server set two cups of coffee on the low table in front of them. "First, I need to apologize to you for any embarrassment I might have caused you at Nanna's party. I know you don't like people talking about you or Dad unless it's in a positive light, and I'm guessing my actions weren't very flattering to you."

Marcia added sugar and cream to her coffee and stirred it slowly as she spoke. "They were not. I'm still getting messages from family members, asking me what was wrong with you. I hope you find time in your busy schedule to go and apologize to your grandmother."

"Tell them they can ask me if they have questions." Chance took a sip from his mug. "Nanna and I have already spoken several times since the party. That is the second reason I asked to see you." Chance reached into his messenger bag and pulled out a manila file filled with papers. "Nanna has asked me to join the board of directors for the Edwards Foundation, and I accepted." He smiled at her. "You're looking at the new Director of Development."

"Wait—" Marcia's face twisted in confusion. "She made you a... director on the foundation's board? Without our approval?"

Chance tapped the folder. "According to my understanding of the bylaws, as director and chief executive of the foundation, she doesn't need board approval. But let's face it, who would object? You've wanted me more involved for years."

Marcia stammered, "Well, yes but—you're busy. You're always busy, isn't that what you said? Isn't that why you wanted me to meet you*here*today, in your neighborhood, instead of coming to the club?"

"Yes, I'm already overwhelmed at the idea of taking on a responsibility of this size. But she made an excellent case on why the position was right for me, and I'm hoping I can help her make the changes that she wants to see."

"Might I ask—" Marcia's tone went icy cold. "What changes are those?"

Chance took another sip, then set his mug down. "She'd like more direct community outreach, a more responsive approach to helping local neighborhoods in need. Also, she's asked me to take the lead in working with two groups very near and dear to both of our hearts—the gay community and animal rescue."

Marcia's face froze. "She asked you to—"

"Yes." Chance's fingers gripped the folder as he tried not to show how scared he was at this moment. It wasn't just that his mother had held sway over his life for so long, but the Edwards foundation was her life. As angry as she made him at times, she was still his mother and he honestly didn't want them to fight over this. "This is important to her, and I assure you, I didn't ask for this or—"

"Oh no, you never wanted this—at least not when I asked for your help. But I suppose this turn of events pleased your boyfriend. I'm surprised you don't have him here to gloat over your victory over me."

Chance tossed the papers on the table in front of them, almost spilling his coffee. "Why do you have to make this about you? I'm not doing this to hurt you, nor does Nanna care if you're happy or not." He exhaled slow and recalled Roz's words about being honest and letting people in. "And, as a matter of fact, I haven't seen Luke since the party."

Marcia tilted her head at Chance and folded her hands in her lap. "I'm sorry to hear that."

"Are you?" he asked.

Marcia took a deep breath. "Your happiness has always been what mattered the most to me. Everything I've said or done has been with your best interest in mind, whether or not you believe it."

Chance made a soft sound. "At a certain point, Mom, I just wanted you to listen to me, and trust my judgment."

"That's hard to do sometimes with your children," she said, and gave him a small smile. "God willing, you'll find out one day when you have kids of your own."

A family of his own. Did he want that? Did Luke? "Maybe one day we'll find out."

• • • • • • • • • •

On Saturday morning, Chance swung by Nolan's apartment and picked him and Diego up to help with the rescue's fund raiser and adoption drive. Once they got to the park, they helped set up two large white canopies and a couple long tables while other volunteers brought cages and crates and assembled holding pens for the animals who'd be arriving soon.

Chance wore his scrubs so they could easily identify him as medical staff in case any potential adopters had questions. He also wore a tall rainbow hat being sold by the Pride Center booth, a hat that Nolan tried several times to steal off his head.

Just after eleven, music started playing nearby. Diego and his band always brought in a good crowd, and they hoped some of those people would wander over and take a look at the cats and dogs up for adoption. He was watching them play when he felt a hand on his shoulder. "I told you, if you want a hat of your own, just go get—"

But it wasn't Nolan.

"Hello, Doctor Chance." Luke held a small fluffy terrier mix in his hands. "How are you?" he asked in that calm voice of his.

"I'm good. And you?" Chance asked, his mouth suddenly dry.

Luke smiled. "I am well, thank you for asking." He glanced down at the curious dog. "This is Britta."

"Hello, Britta." Chance touched her head and smiled. Then his eyes found Luke's. "How are you doing?" he asked and tried to push down the lump in his throat.

"I am well. Jessica asked me to help set up for the adoption drive. By the way, thank you for helping her with the job."

"All I did was put in a good word." He pointed at a tent where the women in charge stood, overseeing the set-up. "Those ladies over there did the rest."

Luke tilted his head at Chance with a knowing smirk. "I doubt they would have been able to do it without their generous benefactor."

Chance shrugged. "It's all for a good cause." He wanted to pull Luke aside and tell him about the foundation and his new role, and how he might have the opportunity to make real change in their communities. He wanted to pull Luke aside and kiss him. But he'd ruined that chance for happiness between them. He shifted from one foot to the next as he spoke. "Luke, I'm sorry for what happened. My actions at Nanna's party were inexcusable."

But Luke shook his head. "There's no need for you to apologize. You said nothing that wasn't true."

Chance stared at Luke. "How can you say that? Aren't you angry with me?"

Luke shrugged. "I was upset at first, but the more I thought about it, the more ridiculous it seemed. We'd been out on two dates, Chance. You owed me nothing but your friendship, which is exactly what you stated to your grandmother."

"No. No, Luke, you are much, much dearer to me than just a friend, and I should have been clearer with everyone there who you were and what you meant to me, especially my grandmother." Chance rubbed his forehead with his hand. "She was mad at me, yes, but not for the reason you'd think. I'd like to tell you the story about it sometime if you'll let me. There's so much I want to tell you." Chance glanced down at his feet before looking back up. "I miss you."

A long moment passed before Luke answered, his voice almost a whisper. "I miss you too. I overreacted because I don't know how to deal with these situations." His face wrinkled as he spoke. "It just reinforced to me I'm not good with other people."

Chance bit his lip. "You were great with me. I've never met anyone like you, and every morning I wake up, I hope that it'll be the day that we find each other again, because we belong together." Chance wanted to pull Luke into his arms and hug him tight, kiss that worried expression off his face. But he couldn't rush this—it had to be when Luke was ready. "I get that I moved way too fast and hurried things, and I'm sorry." Chance reached over and rested his hand on top of Luke's arm. "But if you're willing to take a chance on Doctor Chance, I'll be here waiting for you."

Luke gasped, then laughed aloud, and Chance thought it was the best sound in the world. "How long have you been waiting to use that line?"

Chance chuckled. "Um, seventh grade, maybe? I've been waiting for the right time."

"And I was the lucky recipient." Luke turned his head. Jessica had called his name and beckoned him toward her. "I need to go now," he said, and held up the terrier.

"Of course. But can I call you later?" Chance asked.

Four of the longest seconds of Chance's life passed by, before Luke nodded. "I'd like that. Have a splendid afternoon."

Yes. Those butterflies fluttered again inside Chance's stomach at the sight of Luke's crooked smile. "You too, Luke."

Chapter Twenty-five

The following Thursday, Luke sat in his living room and looked down at his phone.

Six thirty-four PM.

Since they reconnected at the park, they had spoken each night before they went to sleep and talked about their respective days. But then Chance had asked him to go out with him Thursday evening, but not to ask questions about it. "It'll be a great surprise, you'll see." Chance instructed him to be ready for a night of fun and excitement but refused to say more than that. "Do you trust me?" he'd asked Luke, to which Luke replied, "Of course."

Now, he was having regrets.

Six thirty-six PM.

At six thirty-seven, Chance's Tahoe pulled up into the driveway, and Luke stepped outside and locked the door behind him. "Hello," Luke said as he stepped into the passenger side of Chance's car.

"Hi there. You look great," Chance said, and reached his hand out. "Jess out for the evening?"

"I think so." She had said nothing to Luke about any plans, but her car had been gone all afternoon. "Did you have a good day at the clinic?"

"It wasn't very exciting today, but sometimes those are the best days. Just got to spend time with the little creatures." Luke tried to figure out where they were going, but he didn't recognize the route Chance took—until he exited the freeway and headed toward the megaplex movie theater. "Um, Chance?"

Chance grinned and reached for Luke's hand again. "So, a little birdie told me you like Planet Zombie, and I found out that there was a new movie that they just made. Tonight's the premiere, did you know that?"

Luke's heart beat faster, but not in a good way. *Please, no, Chance.* "I had heard about it," Luke said, forcing his voice to stay calm. "I thought that I'd go—"

"You thought you'd have to wait a few weeks, right? Once everyone and their mother's seen it, and all the good plot lines are spoiled?"

Luke took slow deep breaths, preparing himself for the throngs of moviegoers, all excited and dressed up for the opening night of a popular movie. Chance meant well; Luke knew that.

But when Chance turned the corner into the theater's parking lot, Luke's eyes went wide.

It was empty.

Well, not completely empty. Seven vehicles—including Jessica's Explorer and Maggie's minivan—were parked in the lot. "Where is everyone?"

"Well, I don't know, but they're not here." Chance parked and turned off the engine. "It's just us... and some friends. That sound okay?"

Luke stared at him. "You rented out the entire building? All the theaters?"

Now Chance's eyes went wide. "Well, when you say it like that..." They got out of the car and headed for the entrance. Sure enough, the lobby was empty, aside for a security guard talking to what looked like the supervisor, and a couple staff members behind the concession stand. "Popcorn and a soda?" Chance asked.

Luke nodded mutely as the kids at the concession stand handed him their snacks. He kept looking around the empty lobby. "I don't want to know how much this cost." Renting an entire multiplex theater on the opening night of one of the most anticipated movies of the year? "It had to cost—"

Chance shook his head. "Oh, please don't do the math. It's distressing beyond words, and I'll probably never make a grand gesture that costs this much again in my entire life, so don't get used it." But the smile on Chance's face told Luke that he loved every moment of this. "C'mon, let's go."

"We're not late, are we?" Luke asked.

"Baby, they're not starting until you say 'Go.'" Chance leaned in to kiss Luke's cheek. He pulled two tickets out of his jeans and handed them to a ticket agent, who grinned at them and held the door open to the theater with the largest screen in the entire movie theater complex. "This way, gentlemen."

Luke and Chance walked up the dark hallway and turned the corner. No, the theater wasn't completely empty. Over on the center right side, he spotted Jessica sitting next to a friend of hers, and a few rows behind her was her rescue friend Maggie with two teenage boys. Up along the top row was Gigi and another woman who'd dressed up as one of the main characters, and in the row in front of them sat Norma with her husband and kids. There were a few other people Luke didn't know personally, but he recognized from the rescue, and friends of Chance. But everyone was so spread out, each group had their privacy bubbles and as much space as they wanted.

Luke turned back to Chance. "You did this—" But he didn't know what else to say. Luke was speechless.

"C'mon, hurry up," Jessica called out from across the theater. "I wanna see the movie!" A couple other people clapped and laughed, as Luke found two seats near the center, away from the others. Soon the lights went out, and the movie trailers began to roll. Luke took Chance's hand

and pulled it up to his lips, tasting the salt and butter from the popcorn.

Oh yes, he trusted this man with his heart and soul—and every other part of his body.

• • • • • • • • • •

"Did you notice during the second post-credit scene that one of the zombies was holding a pencil." Luke's thoughts outpaced his ability to speak, and he waved his hands frantically. "A pencil!"

"They're doing Zombie Enlightenment for the sequel, that has to be it." Twenty minutes after the movie ended, almost everyone had said their goodbyes and left the theater, but Luke and Miguel, one of Norma's teenaged sons, were still chatting enthusiastically about the film. Miguel grinned. "That's my favorite side quest. Honestly, it could be an entire movie just on its own."

"No doubt." Luke nodded and his face broke out into a matching wide smile. "I wonder who they'll cast as The Professor." Turning to Chance, he noted a bemused expression on his handsome face. "It's a fantastic side quest. A small group zombies retain their knowledge of their previous lives, but don't remember who they were."

"Sounds fun." Chance's arm fell comfortably over Luke's shoulder. "You about ready?" The theater staff had already cleaned up after the small group and were waiting for them to leave so they could go home.

Luke looked over and saw that Norma's family was also waiting for them to finish. "Of course." He and Miguel exchanged Discord handles so they could continue their discussion online, and they all walked out into the empty parking lot. "Thanks again for inviting us," Miguel said to Chance. "I'll never forget this."

They got into Chance's Tahoe and buckled in. "So… did you want to go back to my place tonight?" Chance asked as he started the engine and drove out of the parking lot. "Or do you need to sleep at your house tonight."

Luke frowned. "I do have an early online meeting. They're in Boston, which is an hour earlier than us." But Luke wasn't ready for this magical night to be over. Maybe he was ready to make a grand gesture of his own. "Perhaps you could stay over at my house tonight?"

Chance snapped his head in Luke's direction. "Um, yeah. Are you sure?" Since they'd began dating, all of the nights they'd spent together had been at Chance's apartment.

"Yes."

The rest of the drive was quiet, but Chance reached for Luke's hand and held it as they drove.

They entered the dark house, and Luke turned on a lamp in the living room as their Waylon and Willie, their current fosters, trotted downstairs to greet them. "Can I get you something to drink?" Luke asked, and headed into the kitchen.

"Water, please." Chance glanced up the stairs, and his eyes narrowed at the sound of noise coming from the second floor. "I didn't see Jessica's car."

"She leaves her television on for them. Nature videos mostly, but Waylon likes The Weather Channel." Luke handed Chance a bottle of water. "You've never seen my room, have you?"

Chance shook his head. "Not in person." They'd video chatted a few times, but this really was another first for them. "I'm curious to see your office."

Luke took Chance's hand, and led him upstairs, pointing out Jessica's room and the bathroom. "This is me," he said, and opened his door, displaying a relatively tidy room—thank goodness he'd made his bed that morning. But a nervous tension pooled in his belly. He couldn't remember the last time *anyone* had been here aside from Jess, and never a lover, never anyone who spent the night. This room was Luke's domain, his safe space, his retreat from the world since he was six years old. Chance took it all in, from the cluttered desk to the graphic novels piled next to Luke's bed, to the posters hanging on his wall—a blueprint of the Millennium Falcon from Star Wars next to a similar poster with the Starship Enterprise from Star Trek. "What do you think?" Luke asked as he sat down on his bed, his hands folded in front of him.

Chance sat next to him and pointed at the posters. "You're missing the Battlestar Galactica, but other than that, it's pretty cool in here."

Luke stared for a moment, then realized that Chance was teasing him. "I'll see what I can do to rectify that—" But Chance had leaned in to steal a kiss, and Luke's hands lifted to cradle Chance's face. They kissed for a few minutes until Willie jumped on his bed, followed soon by Waylon. Unacceptable. "Oh no, beasts. Out." He stood and gently shooed them out of this room and closed the door behind him. When he turned around, Chance began unbuttoning his shirt, and those nerves dissipated. How could he ever have been scared of this? "Um—I don't have any condoms here in my room. I could text my sister and ask if she has any."

But Chance shook his head. "Don't worry about it. I just want to hold you." His hands reached out, and Luke walked toward him, standing between Chance's legs. He looked down at that beloved face, and his fingers threaded through that golden hair.

Was this love? Luke thought so, and it was unlike anything he'd ever experienced. "Thank you for the movie." His fingertips traveled down the curves and planes of Chance's face, memorizing each pore and freckle. Then they moved south and tugged the shirt off of Chance's shoulders, watching it slip down onto the bed. Chance's chest was smooth and golden, like the rest of his body, and Luke wasn't sure how long he stood there, just touching his lover's skin.

Then Chance pulled him down onto the bed, and there was no more need for words.

Chapter Twenty-six

"Hold on." Gigi marched out of the break room, her voice loud and indignant as she held an empty takeout bag. "Someone went to Sumo Sushi and didn't let me know?" Standing with her hands on her hips, she frowned. "I thought we were friends, people. *I thought we were family.*"

Norma snorted and nudged Chance, who sat next to her as they finished suturing a Siamese cat's front leg. "I don't eat that stuff, so I guess we know who hurt you like that."

"Why, Doctor Chance?" Gigi's voice wavered theatrically. "Haven't I been good to you?" Then both women began laughing. "Or maybe someone else has been even better?"

Chance arched a brow. "I ended up staying later than usual last night, and Luke swung by and brought me some dinner out of the kindness of his heart." That Luke stayed the night wasn't anything that they needed to know, but the smile on his face spoke volumes about how he felt. "I'll remember to ask for extra next time I see him."

Gigi smirked. "Or I can mention it later. He'll be here for the ribbon cutting, right?"

Right. Chance chuckled and finished stitching up the cat's leg. "Yes, I believe so. He's coming with his sister." Ever since the festival in the park, Dani and Jessica had become fast friends. Everyone in the rescue appeared to be thrilled with Jessica's energy and drive and had given her full reins in prepping the office for its grand opening, which would take place later that afternoon in their new office next door to the vet clinic, newly vacant after the dog groomers moved down the street.

Gigi winked at Chance and headed back to the front of the clinic. Norma caught Chance's eye as they lifted the sleeping dog. "And your mother?" she asked.

Chance hesitated. "I'm not sure. The donation of the office space for an animal rescue organization is a huge boon to the community. We'll have media here, and getting the Edwards Foundation in the news has always been something she's been invested in." He stroked the sleeping cat. "I hope she comes."

Norma squeezed his shoulder. "Me too."

Once Clara arrived for the afternoon shift, Chance left and headed upstairs to change. They'd booked light that afternoon so Chance could step out and take part in the ribbon cutting ceremony. While he didn't relish most of the managerial duties that came with being the director of development, Chance looked forward to being there today to share this great day with the rescue.

Sheba sat on the bed and watched Chance struggle with his tie. "This is funny to you?" he asked as those green eyes followed his fingers. Just then, a rap at the front door spooked Sheba, and he jumped up and ran off.

It was Luke and Jessica. Chance had left the lower door unlocked so they could park in the back and walk up to his studio when they arrived. "Hey there," Chance said, and opened the door wider to they could enter. "You guys ready?"

Luke nodded while Jessica walked around, her mouth agape. "This is even more cool than Luke made it sound. Wow." Her eyes darted everywhere. "Very impressive, Doctor Chance."

"Glad you like it." Chance leaned over and kissed Luke's cheek. "You look nice," he said, and glanced approvingly at the button-down shirt and chinos Luke wore. "I see Jessica's taken you shopping again."

"Such a chore." Jessica flicked a stray piece of dog hair off Luke's shirt. "Had to make sure he looked presentable."

Luke frowned. "I am standing right here."

"Yes, you are, handsome." Chance reached for Luke's hand, and they fit together, like two pieces of a puzzle.

How had he ever gone so long without this kind of touch in his life? "How are things looking downstairs?" he asked.

Jessica's face broke out into a wide grin. "I dare you to find an animal rescue with a better-looking office. We've got information for volunteers and some merchandise examples in the window with the new logo." They'd discovered that Maggie, Jessica's rescue buddy, had some background experience in graphic design and she redesigned the rescue's trademark rainbow logo. It looked sharper, more professional, and everyone loved it. "I expect you both to order decals for your cars."

Luke frowned, but Chance just laughed. "Consider it done."

Another knock at his door surprised them all—Chance hadn't asked anyone else to come up and see him. He blinked fast as he opened it. "Mom—Nanna?"

Marcia looked downcast, but she was clearly dressed for a day in front of the press, in a smart peach colored suit and matching heels. Chance was glad to see her, despite their differences. But it was his grandmother's presence that shocked him. "What are you doing here?" he asked and hugged them both as they entered his apartment.

"A little bird told me that today was a special day for the foundation, and I didn't want to miss it." Once inside, Chance introduced Luke and Jessica to his mother and grandmother.

Marcia nodded and kept her cool composure, but her curiosity was hard to miss. Nanna reached for Jessica's hand. "Are you the young lady I've been speaking with on the phone?" she asked, and when Jessica nodded, they stepped aside and began to talk.

"I'm glad you're here," Chance said to his mother. "I didn't think you'd make it."

Marcia snorted. It was a sound Chance rarely heard from her. "I tried to resign from the foundation. Evelyn wouldn't let me." They glanced over at the older woman talking animatedly to Jessica. "She said there are things I need to learn first from my son, so—" Marcia raised her hands. "I'm here to learn. And you must be Luke. I'm glad to meet you under better circumstances," she added, and offered her hand.

How much of this change of heart in his mother was real and how much of it was Nanna's threats? Chance didn't know, but right now, he also didn't care.

Luke took the hand with a deferential nod. "Likewise. To be honest, we should have first done this in a more private environment."

Marcia was stunned. "That's exactly what I said, but—"

They both looked at Chance, who held up his hands. "I learned my lesson. From now on, I will listen to you both before making any serious decisions." Just then Nanna walked over and caught Luke's hands with surprising alacrity. "It's good to meet you, Luke. I hope we'll be able to spend some time together later this evening."

"Yes ma'am," Luke answered with his shy smile.

"We'll head downstairs to get ready. See you soon!" Jessica said and pulled Luke with her.

Chance watched them go, then turned back to his mother and grandmother. "Do you want to sit down? I've got water and lemonade in the fridge."

"Either would be fine," his grandmother said, but Marcia shook her head. Chance poured two glasses of lemonade and set one in front of Evelyn. "I'm glad you're here."

"Libby told me I needed to get out more, so here I am. Also, I wanted to talk to both of you, someplace private." Evelyn reached for Marcia's hand. "My dear, we have not always gotten along, but you're a good wife to my dolt of a son, and one of the smartest women I've ever met."

Marcia raised a single eyebrow. Chance choked on his lemonade.

Next, Evelyn took Chance's hand. "You two need each other if you're going to fix my charitable foundation. Marcia has the mind for juggling the numbers and pressing the flesh, but not a shred of compassion for the people she needs to help. Chance, learn everything you can about this from her. Don't waste a minute being resentful and petty. Teach her how to understand these people who we're helping." She sought out his eyes, holding them in her gaze. "But let her know you as well. You've kept everyone at arm's length your entire life, then wonder why no one understands you."

Chance looked at his mother. *Had he done that?* Had he unilaterally decided that they wouldn't understand him and built that wall around himself? "I will, Nanna. And... I'm sorry, Mom."

Marcia covered her face with her hands and took a deep breath. "I'm sorry as well. I mean well, even if it doesn't appear that way. And I know that you're a grown man now and I can't run every detail of your life anymore. I *am* proud of you, you know."

Chance steepled his fingers in front of him. "I didn't know."

Evelyn sighed. "She just said it, Chance, what more do you want. Give and take, both of you, before it's too late." She pointed a finger at them. "But you two need to get my foundation back in line, and giving money to the right people, or—" She cackled and rubbed her hands together. "Or I'll leave it all to Libby, every cent. Just watch me."

• • • • • • • • • •

"And with that, we'd like to welcome you into End of the Rainbow Rescue's official headquarters. Cutting the ribbon today is our generous benefactor, Evelyn Brightwell Edwards, Executive Director of the Edwards Charitable Foundation," Roxanne Parker Miranda held out one end of the wide rainbow ribbon, and her wife Ella held the other as Nanna used an oversized pair of scissors to cut it in two.

Chance waited until most of the assembled group—mostly rescue volunteers, but also some bloggers and a local television station—were inside before he entered. It really looked fantastic. They had filled the walls with posters of their current animals awaiting adoption along with some success stories, pictures of dogs and cats with smiling families.

His eyes darted around the room until he spotted Luke, who stood next to his grandmother in front of a large, framed portrait on the back wall. "—and all he had to do was whistle, and that squirrel would skitter down from whatever branch he was on and run up to Travis." She stopped when she saw Chance join them. "Cricket, look at this."

Chance studied the photograph hanging on the wall, a laughing man standing next to a sleek brown horse, his smile so much like his grandmother's—and maybe his own—aimed back at him from across the years.

Below the picture was a wooden plaque affixed to the wall, under a box displaying military awards.

We dedicate this chapter of End of the Rainbow Rescue to Corporal Travis Brightwell, animal lover and military hero.

There were other photographs of Travis with dogs, cats, and Chance recognized his grandmother as a young girl in a few of them. He took Nanna's hand in his and held it carefully. "This is incredible. I'm glad you got to see this."

"Me too," she whispered. "Jessica helped me find more photographs and set all of this up." She sighed and leaned against Chance. "He would love everything that you are doing here with this rescue group. Of course, he'd want to transport the dogs on the back of his horse," she added with a chuckle.

Luke snorted, and all three of them laughed. Out of the corner of his eye, Chance saw his mother speaking with the reporter from the local news station, her face animated as she waved a hand around the building.

Evelyn noticed. "Let her help you with this stuff, Chance. She'll argue, but that's okay. Don't just avoid her because you don't want to fight. Tell her how you want the foundation to go, and she'll make it happen. But no good comes from just ignoring your problems." She turned to Luke. "Now you, young man. Explain to me again what kinds of apps you make? Can you put one on my phone?" she asked, as they walked toward the front of the office.

Chance looked up once more at his great-uncle Travis, who'd been born in the wrong time and place. Chance had lucked into being born into privilege and comfort, and would never, ever take that for granted again.

Chapter Twenty-seven

L uke wandered downstairs and into the kitchen to grab a snack before his three PM video conference with Russell and his team. The travelogue app was all done and had gone through Luke's final checks. From what he'd heard, Russell's bosses loved Luke's work and were already talking about contracting Luke for their next big app idea.

Jessica sat at the kitchen table, her laptop open in front of her. "Thank you again for the birthday check, Aunt Linda. I'm going shopping later today with some friends for new work clothes."

His aunt's voice drifted out of the speakers. "An office manager is an important job, Jessie, especially for a non-profit group. You must look professional if you want to attract the big donations. Are you dragging Luke with you?"

Jessica snorted. "Oh, I should, but then I'd spend the whole time trying to spruce up his meager wardrobe." She stopped and watched as Luke strolled into the kitchen. "Speak of the devil—"

Luke rolled his eyes as he passed behind Jessica and waved at his aunt over Jessica's shoulder. "Hello there."

Linda beamed at him from the laptop screen. "There he is. We were just talking about you and your young man, and what a wonderful contribution his family has made to that rescue organization that Jessica's working for now. She tells me they've got her pretty busy with volunteer wrangling."

"From what I gather, there is no end to the work that needs to be done." He rested one hand on Jessica's shoulder. "Did she tell you about her latest project?"

"The Snip-Snipmobile?" Jessica said with a chuckle. "I think we can blame Chance for at least fifty percent of that idea. But just imagine—if we could get a mobile surgical van into the communities and work directly with the families and offer low-cost or free spays and neuters, what a difference it would make to those neighborhoods." Chance had already offered any help she needed getting it set up, and already had veterinarian friends of his volunteering to work with them.

"She told me all about it," Aunt Linda answered, her eyes darting between the two of them. "I'm very proud of her. Of both of you."

Jessica looked down at her phone. "Aunt Linda, my ride's here to pick me up. It was good talking to you!" Jessica winked at Luke, grabbed her purse from the kitchen table, and headed out the door.

"She looks happy," Aunt Linda said, as her eyes scanned Luke, who sat down in the chair in front of the laptop. "You look happy too, dear."

Luke considered her statement. "I am. Better than content, if that makes sense."

"It does. And thank you for sending me those pictures from the fund raiser last weekend. It was good to see you out and about with your young man."

He chuckled to himself, as he always did when Aunt Linda called Chance 'his young man.' "It was a stroke of genius, having the Pride Center hold a pet adoption drive. Both organizations could share their message with the community." Even better, Chance could spend time with both groups and didn't feel as if he short-changed anyone, particularly Luke, who sat next to him for part of the time.

"Well, I just enjoyed seeing you out of the house, and not stuck in your bedroom."

There was that too. "Of course. Then you'll be glad to hear that I'm going to Galveston next weekend with my young man. Chance's grandmother wants him to help her re-organize the family's foundation operating guidelines and look at the upcoming budgets with the other directors." Roslyn had offered to join them for the weekend and spend time with Luke while Chance was occupied, and Luke looked forward to that more than he'd expected.

"Chance sounds like a very busy man. I hope I get to meet him soon," Aunt Linda said.

"About that—Jessica and I talked the other evening about hosting Thanksgiving here at our home and inviting our friends over, especially the ones who don't have any place to go." People from the Pride Center, new friends from the Rainbow rescue group, all their co-workers, and whoever else could make it.

Luke had learned that crowds weren't as daunting when they were friends. A lesson he was learning late, but better late than never.

Aunt Linda's face lit up. "That sounds great. I love that."

"The first step is some redecorating." Luke looked around the kitchen and over into the living room. "This house is a memorial to the late twentieth century. We're going to buy some new furniture and maybe paint the walls." A wry smile crossed his face. "Perhaps a better set up for the dogs."

Aunt Linda nodded. "I'm glad to hear that. Let me know if you need any money from the trust, and I'll send it over."

"Thank you. Better yet—Jessica and I hoped you might come down and visit us." Luke's smile was shy, but genuine. "I'd like you to meet Chance."

Her eyes misted up. "I'd love to, Luke. Thank you for the invitation. We'll talk more about it when we get closer to the holidays." Now it was Aunt Linda's turn to glance at her phone. "Goodness, I've been just chatting on and on here. I've got to run, but I'll talk to you soon. Goodbye, dear boy."

The video call ended, and Luke closed Jessica's laptop. He glanced around the kitchen, a room that hadn't changed in at least fifteen years, maybe longer. Yes, it was time to update this place. Just like the apps he worked with—everything needed an occasional update.

His phone vibrated as he put together a quick sandwich for lunch. Luke swiped the screen, then grinned at the photograph Chance sent him. He was at the clinic, in his blue scrubs, kneeling behind Sadie, who was licking his face.

> Chance: *Look who came to see me today? She's doing great and looks healthy. Her foster mom says she's walking on her own. Might be a foster-fail situation here. [smiley face emoji]*
> Chance: *Our girl's got a bright future.*

Luke smiled and touched the screen. All three of them had come so far from that day.

His phone pinged again.

Chance: *Can't wait to see you tonight.*

Luke: *Me too.*

Luke closed the phone and set it in his pocket. If he wanted to spend the night with Chance (and he did), he needed to finish today's to-do list. He grabbed his sandwich, a soft drink, and headed upstairs.

The future did indeed look bright.

Argentina Ryder spent her early career as a high school teacher in Texas, sharing her love of geography and traveling with her students. After completing her masters in education, she worked as a curriculum and instruction consultant while working on her first novel.

Argentina's bucket list includes visiting all the national parks and running a ten-minute mile. She spends free time in her garden, kayaking Texas rivers, and littering her house with various DIY projects. Her red slider, Pebbles, enjoys frozen strawberries, basking under her UV light, and spending quality time outside on sunny days while Lucrezia, her Siamese, mostly just sleeps.

She lives with her family and her pets and is currently working on the next books in her *Paws and Claws* and *Rio Riendo* series. Sign up for her newsletter at argentinaryder.com to keep up with what's going on in her world and get sneak peeks at what's coming up.